"I'M TURNING YOU OVER TO JOSEPH PAYNE BRENNAN. JUST FOR GOD'S SAKE DON'T LET GO OF HIS ARM!"

— STEPHEN KING

DIARY OF A WEREWOLF

April 26, 1958: I feel a sudden sense of exhilaration, of release . . . yet it terrifies me. Is it possible the heroin has damaged the higher centers of my brain? I fear the drug has triggered an atavistic urge deep within me, buried but still smouldering . . .

As I run, I become a wild animal—which all of us essentially are. Worries and cares become nonexistent. I live completely and fully in the moment. I feel that I have thoroughly adapted myself. Now I must begin to hunt. . . .

The Shapes of Midnight

Horror by

JOSEPH PAYNE BRENNAN

THE SHAPES OF MIDNIGHT

HORROR BY
JOSEPH PAYNE BRENNAN

WITH AN
INTRODUCTION BY
STEPHEN KING

B

BERKLEY BOOKS, NEW YORK

THE SHAPES OF MIDNIGHT

A Berkley Book / published by arrangement with
the author

PRINTING HISTORY
Berkley edition / October 1980

ISBN: 0-425-04567-6

A BERKLEY BOOK® TM 757,375

PRINTED IN THE UNITED STATES OF AMERICA

ACKNOWLEDGEMENTS

Diary of a Werewolf, copyright 1961 by Joseph Payne Brennan for *Macabre*, Number VIII, Winter 1960.

The Corpse of Charlie Rull, copyright 1959 by Joseph Payne Brennan, for *The Dark Returners*.

Canavan's Back Yard, copyright 1958 by Joseph Payne Brennan, for *Nine Horrors and a Dream*.

The Pavilion, copyright 1959 by Joseph Payne Brennan, for *The Dark Returners*.

House of Memory, copyright 1967 by H. S. D. Publications, Inc., for *Alfred Hitchcock's Mystery Magazine*, September 1969.

The Willow Platform, copyright 1973 by Stuart David Schiff for *Whispers Magazine*.

Who Was He?, copyright 1969 by H. S. D. Publications, Inc., for *Alfred Hitchcock's Mystery Magazine*, September 1969.

Disappearance, copyright 1959 by Joseph Payne Brennan, for *The Dark Returners*.

The Horror at Chilton Castle, copyright 1963 by Joseph Payne Brennan, for *Scream at Midnight*.

The Impulse to Kill, copyright 1959 by Joseph Payne Brennan, for *The Dark Returners*.

The House on Hazel Street, copyright 1961 by Joseph Payne Brennan, for *Macabre*, Number IX, Summer 1961.

Slime, copyright 1953 by Weird Tales, for *Weird Tales*, March 1953.

CONTENTS

Introduction
for
THE SHAPES OF MIDNIGHT

By Stephen King

Hey, I want to tell you something funny . . . and you better listen.

The *reason* you better listen is that you are holding Joseph Payne Brennan's new collection of short stories in your hands, and pretty soon you're going to start to read them, and soon after that night is going to fall (or maybe, worse luck for you, it has already fallen), and believe me, dear friend, believe your old Uncle Stevie: When night comes and you are in the middle of Joe Brennan's latest—and long over-due—collection of ghastly family snapshots, you may find you *need* something funny to hold onto. Like a lifeline.

So here is the something funny: They *paid* me to do this introduction.

Not much, that is true. Enough, maybe, to pay for two visits from the television repairman or one from the plumber; enough for a week's groceries (if my kids are having a picky week, that is); or maybe enough to buy a cord and a half of wood for the Better 'n Ben's woodstove we run out of our fireplace.

In other words, not much . . . but they *paid* me.

Poor old Berkley Books.

Shall I tell you how I earned my money? Why not—no secrets among friends, right? This is how I did it: I took the manuscript of THE SHAPES OF MIDNIGHT, sent to me by Joe's editor at Berkley, John Silbersack, and I put it on a small endtable by the stove. I pulled a six-pack of Black Label beer out of the icebox and plonked it down next to the script. I drew up *my* chair—the one I read in, the rocker with the faded tartan upholstery—next to the endtable and plonked myself down in the chair. I took up the manuscript.

Then, dear friends, I read for four solid hours.

I killed the six-pack. I killed the evening. The only thing I didn't kill was time, because you can only do that if you're screwing around and doing something you really don't give a tin whistle about. And in this case, nothing could have been further from such a situation.

Night falls early in western Maine, and the sun disappears with an almost tropical suddenness behind the bulk of the White Mountains. The wind picks up and the lake funnels it between its high, sloping sides. It keens around the eaves like a woman who has been lost long and hopelessly . . . or like a beast whining for entry. It is a depthless sound, wintry and dark and merciless, a sound that seems to demand a flickering fire, a few cold beers . . . and the voice of a master storyteller. I supplied the fire, stoked with good dry maple, and a Massachusetts brewery supplied the brew. It was Joseph Payne Brennan who supplied the final precious ingredient, may he live forever and may his tribe increase; it was Joseph Payne Brennan who supplied the voice, who brought me the words in the wind, riding over the darkness. And when I finish off blowing my bazoo here, he may do it for you. If you're ready.

Listen, just for a minute, to the voice of a master of the unashamed horror tale:

"It was a great gray-black hood of horror moving over the floor of the sea. It slid through the soft ooze like a monstrous mantle of slime obscenely animated with questing life . . . It was animated by a single, unceasing, never-satisfied drive: a voracious, insatiable hunger . . ."

I first read those words some twenty years ago, encountering them in a paperback anthology from the late '50s—was it *Zacherley's Vulture Stew*? I almost think that it may have been, little that it matters now. What matters is the *frisson* they brought to a boy of twelve, sitting cross-legged and bug-eyed under the reading lamp over his bed, a boy who was wearing nothing but a pair of Haines underpants and a lot of gooseflesh. There are times when you know you are in the hands of a storyteller working at the height of his powers, and those are rare and wonderful moments to be treasured—among my own I number my first reading of Mark Twain's *Tom Sawyer*, Bram Stoker's *Dracula*, Harlan Ellison's "The Sound of a Scythe". . . and Joseph Payne Brennan's classic story of right-out, right-on horror, "Slime." Later—much later—I bought an issue of *Weird Tales* (at a scalper's price, he grumbled with typical New England parsimony) which featured the story—it was featured in the March, 1953 issue, for the record—but not even the cover art and interior heading by the great Virgil Finlay could do the story credit. A picture is worth a thousand words, they say . . . but in this case, words overwhelm the artist's pen. Not even Virgil Finlay could catch the essence of that obscene, rolling hood of slime coughed up from the ocean's floor. It is between you and Joe, dear reader—between his imagination and yours. It is one of the classic novellas in this field, and even if you happen to be perusing this tome in the middle of a July heatwave (or on a ship at anchor in Hong Kong Bay, for that matter), you are going to hear—and feel—the winterwhine of a hungry wind under your door.

Joseph Payne Brennan is one of the most effective writers in the horror genre, and he is certainly one of the writers I have patterned my own career upon; one of the writers whom I studied and with whom I kept school. You will find nothing flashy in his work, none of H.P. Lovecraft's baroque phraseology, none of Lord Dunsany's elegant turns. There is none of what John D. MacDonald calls the "hey look at me, Ma, ain't I writing *nice*?" syndrome in Brennan's work. Neither will you find more than a hint of the Elder Gods or those cyclopean horrors of which Lovecraft and Clark Ashton Smith were so fond. Which is not to say you will not find dark things aplenty, or grue to chill your blood. You will; and if you don't believe me, wait until you make the acquaintance of Charlie Rull, an anonymous tramp who is felled by a fatal heart attack while crossing a cattail swamp near his shack shelter. "Thirty years of cheap whiskey, greasy food, and general physical abuse had finally caught up with him," Brennan tells us, but where many other tales would end, Brennan's begins, and before you have finished with Charlie Rull, you may find you have eaten most of your fingernails.

Brennan writes in what E.B. White called "the plain style," a style which is as modest and as self-effacing as Joe Brennan is himself . . . but for all of that, it is a sturdy style, capable of wielding enormous power when it is used well. As it is here. In fact, THE SHAPES OF MIDNIGHT could serve as an exercise-book for the young writer who aspires to pen and publish his or her own weird tales.

Although "Slime" is quite possibly Brennan's most famous tale, you will find others in here just as good . . . if a story which makes you nervous about turning out the light afterwards fits into your definition of good, that is. How effective can Joe Brennan's plain style be? Well, make the experiment for yourself, if you like; read "The Horror at Chilton Castle" and then try going down cellar without turning the light on. If you make it more than half-way down, you can award yourself The King Medal for Valor in the Face of Darkness. If, on the other hand, you are like me, you may get two or three steps down . . . and begin thinking about that unspeakable thing in the secret room . . . the clink of fetters against stone (and exactly how strong are those fetters after five hundred years? that is the question that haunts when the story has been finished!) . . . and all of a sudden you might decide making popcorn in the kitchen would be a better idea. With all the lights in the house on.

Or let Brennan take you by the hand and lead you to the town of Juniper Hill . . . a pleasant enough rural area on the surface, but definitely not a place you'd want to visit without a competent guide. Juniper Hill is one of those magic places, like Lovecraft's Arkham or Charlie Grant's Oxrun Station where anything can happen . . . and often does. There's something in the woods not far from Hemlock House, something you'd just as soon not meet when the moon is full, I think. Or perhaps you'd like to go across the township and meet Russell Mellmer. You can't meet his brother Dan, unfortunately, because Dan has disappeared. Yet he may turn up before you have finished the tale; yes, he will almost certainly turn up. And if your blood doesn't run cold when he does, I'd have to guess that you've been drinking antifreeze. And then there is

Henry Crotell; your guided tour of the Juniper Hill area wouldn't be complete without meeting Henry, who has discovered a certain old book in the cellar-hole of the old Trobish house. Henry, you will discover, is about to embark on crash courses in Latin and architecture. Worse luck for him . . .

Brennan writes well and truly about country scenes and country people. There is no bogus romanticism here; instead there is the sort of truth of setting and character that perhaps only fantasy can provide. I tell you this a bit reluctantly: although I love the works of H.P. Lovecraft, and although I count such tales as "The Colour Out of Space" and "The Dunwich Horror" among the most frightening stories I have ever read, Lovecraft was a city man at bottom, and Brennan's stories of rural horror and small town grue ring truer to my ear than any of Lovecraft's, who could never have written Henry Crotell's wonderful answer to the narrator's question in "The Willow Platform." How many times a day do you brush your teeth? the narrator, who is impressed by the whiteness and evenness of Henry's choppers, asks. Henry doubles up with silent laughter and replies, "Nary brush! Nary toothpaste!" It is a small moment, but a damned fine one. We believe in Henry Crotell, because he sounds real. The line puts flesh on his bones and we see him a little more clearly. It is a minor magic trick . . . but maybe you can't quantify magic, because so few people can do it. Right?

All right, all right, I'm almost done now. I can sense your impatience just below the politeness you have shown me. You have places to go and things to see . . . but after you see some of them, you may wish you hadn't. There is the pavillion, for instance, so gay in summer with its bathers and its laughter, so grim and shadowed in winter . . . but let Joe tell you. Joe has been there, you see, and he knows about something under the pilings . . . something ghastly . . .

But before I quit, let me add that there is a story in this collection which I consider to be one of the dozen best stories of the macabre ever written by an American, in the genre or out of it. The black hood of horror flowing out the swamp in "Slime" is all very well, and there is certainly something about the seedy little barber in his alpaca coat in "Who Was He?" . . . but it is in a simple back yard full of weeds and overgrown with autumn-dry, brindle-colored grass that you may find the deepest reverberations of terror. You will find no terrible monster in the back yard of Canavan the antiquarian, no walking zombies, no terrible creation of superscience. It's just a back yard, but something is wrong with it. Dreadfully wrong. You'll find out. The only stories which come to mind as equals of Joe Brennan's "Canavan's Back Yard" in terms of cumulative effect and quiet overall success are Charlotte Parkins Gilman's "The Yellow Wallpaper" and William Faulkner's "A Rose for Emily." It is a tale where ultimate horror lies whispering between the lines. And it will linger in your memory, as it has lingered in mine.

There are collections of short stories that are meant to be read not just once but many times; collections which are not to be loaned out (and when someone asks to borrow the book, summon up all your courage and integrity, and scream into the face of the would-be borrower: "BUY YOUR OWN, TURKEY!") lest they be lost forever—such loss to be bitterly regretted in later years. Charles Beaumont's *The Magic Man* is such a collection; Ray Bradbury's *The October Country*; Richard Matheson's *Shock*; Fritz Leiber's *Night's Black Agents*. Here is another, long overdue but finally here.

So turn off the damned television. Drag your chair

a little closer to the fire, even if it's August out there with heat lightning tattooing the sky and mosquitoes whining against the screens. A lot of cold winter chills are waiting for you. I'm through; I'm turning you over to Joseph Payne Brennan.

Just for God's sake don't let go of his arm!

Stephen King
November 20, 1979

Diary
of a
Werewolf

The following appalling document is herewith exposed to public scrutiny, not with any idea of cheap sensationalism, but simply to serve as a warning for those who may at times find themselves subjected to perverse and atavistic impulses—impulses, we are convinced, originating in the Pit of Hell. All such fiendish impulses should be instantly dismissed from mind. The unspeakable creature whose diary follows entertained himself with such an impulse, toyed with it as it were, and finally yielded to it. No words of ours could fittingly describe the subsequent horror. The diary of this savage monster himself is more than adequate.

April 4, 1958: I am now well settled in Hemlock House. The area suits me admirably. The old stone farm house, surrounded by a grove of towering hemlocks, is located in a wild and desolate region not far from the village of Juniper Hill. Three hundred acres of deep woods, pathless swamps, and overgrown fields go with the house. I will have plenty of room to roam around in without trespassing on my neighbors' land. I can scarcely wait to get out and tramp through these lonely forests. It will be so restful!

April 6, 1958: The house is now in order and very shortly I shall begin to explore my holdings. But I must rest first for a day or two. I came here on the advice of my doctor. He warned me that my many "dissipations" would inevitably lead to physical and mental ruin unless I slowed my pace and got more rest. I disregarded his advice until I began to have horrible nightmares, and then actual blackouts. At that point I became thoroughly alarmed and decided my dear doddering old doctor might be right after all. It was not easy to leave my little harem in New York, and I do miss the heroin sessions—one has such visions!—but I'm sure I shall adjust. There is something about this region which intrigues me already—it has primitive, stark, savage aspects which unaccountably attract me. What a change from "the neon jungle"!

April 8, 1958: I spent nearly a whole day prowling the deep woods. I feel rested, and yet strangely excited also. I like the cold light in these woods, the shadows, the silence, the realization that they shelter not a few four-footed hunters on the track of their prey! I can imagine that in a different guise I stalked through just such a wilderness thousands of years ago. The thought of it somehow thrills me. What bizarre fancies I find myself indulging in!

April 11, 1958: I have been out for two days in cold, rainy weather. These great gloomy stretches of forest are like a magnet which irresistibly draws me—to what I know not. I do not even carry a gun, and yet I feel that I am one of the hunters. How absurd!

April 13, 1958: Yesterday I drove into Juniper Hill for supplies. A typical dull, sleepy little village, lost in this wilderness. I was oddly ill at ease in the presence of these country folk. I felt an animosity toward them, almost a hatred. What stupid lives they must lead. And why do they stare at me as if I had two heads? Idiot yokels, nothing more. I am a fool to let them annoy me. And yet I have a perverse impulse to explode their tedious little treadmill into a nightmare.

April 16, 1958: There is one deep stretch of pine forest which particularly attracts me. It is so dark and quiet under those trees. The fallen pine needles of many decades muffle all sound. I spend hours there; it is so restful. At times I sprawl hidden behind a tree and watch to see if anything goes by. I, too, I tell myself, am one of the hunters!

April 20, 1958: I must keep away from the pine forest. Two days ago, while prowling about in that shadowy place, I was suddenly all but overwhelmed by the weirdest impulse. *I wanted to get down on all fours and run through the woods like an animal!* Of course I did not. I came quickly home and got out the brandy bottle. I finally went to bed a bit tipsy.

April 22, 1958: Last night I dreamed that I was running through the pine forest like a wolf, hunting for prey. I shuddered when I woke and remembered, but what really frightens me is that I experienced no fear or revulsion during the dream itself. I experienced, rather, a sense of exhilaration!

April 26, 1958: Today, after three days of tension

and fretfulness, I returned to the pine forest. As I stole about under the trees, my dream seemed more vivid than ever. After much hesitation, I decided it might be amusing—and certainly not harmful—to enact the dream, at least the general idea of it. Hunting out the most shadowy and secluded spot available, I actually got down on all fours and began ambling along over the mounds of pine needles. In the very beginning it seemed absurd and awkward; I was about to stand up. But very quickly my feelings changed. As in the dream, I felt a sudden sense of exhilaration, of release from all sorts of restraints. I seemed to become a different entity. I loped ahead faster, while sudden savage impulses flamed in my brain. I knew at last the ruthless pure joy of the hunter! I longed for the sight of some smaller, cowering creature which I could chase, overtake, and rend apart. I bounded along until exhaustion overcame me; then I staggered home and spent the remainder of the day drinking brandy. I write this with trembling hand. My experience in the pine forest must not be repeated. I swear that I shall stay away.

April 28, 1958: I am exhausted as I pen this, but I must try to keep a record of what is happening to me. In spite of my resolution to the contrary, I went back to the accursed pine forest and ran about under those black trees like a wild beast—*on all fours, growling, snapping, and snarling at I know not what!* My own identity seemed merged in that of some demon thing—a thing that sought its joy in the hunt, in the rending of throats, in the gush of fresh blood! I feel terror-stricken, yet helpless. O God—is it possible that the heroin has damaged my brain?—inflamed, perhaps, certain cerebral cells which have in turn triggered buried but still smouldering atavistic impulses? Or is it a hereditary curse which has finally crept upon me? I have always known that I had abnormally long arms—it is this which permits me to run so well on all fours! What can I do? I must get away. Yes, tomorrow I shall leave.

April 30, 1958: I write this in terror! The thing has a hold on me which I cannot break. I was packed this morning, ready to leave—and then I glanced out of the window toward the silhouette of pine forest, green-black on the near horizon. I left my suitcases standing in the hall; a half hour later I was racing along on all fours under those great silent trees. I shambled back, hours later, and collapsed on my bed.

May 3, 1958: I have now got a hold on myself. I don't mean that I have conquered my impulse to run about on all fours in the pine forest. But I have decided to make the best of the situation—to be philosophical about it. If I am unable to suppress the impulse, I have decided I might as well enjoy it. Perhaps it is merely a temporary derangement which will run its course.

May 9, 1958: The trouble with the pine forest is that it does not actually shelter much prey. It is perhaps too isolated. I may venture into the more lightly timbered areas closer to the open fields. My palms are now quite thoroughly calloused, and I can bound along at a great rate. I am no longer shocked. I feel a sense of release, of soaring exhilaration, of pure, savage, pristine joy which nothing else has ever given me. As I run along, a wild animal (which all of us essentially are) worries and cares become non-existent. I live completely and fully in the moment. I feel that I have thoroughly adapted myself. Now I must begin to hunt. . . .

May 11, 1958: My first attempt at serious hunting

ended in a ludicrous episode. As I was stalking along through a patch of great forest ferns which flourish in the rich soil under these evergreens, I ran straight onto a half-grown black bear. The bear stopped in surprise, stared at me for a moment (head to head; I was on all fours the same as he), and then backed away. I squatted down and roared with wild laughter. This seemed to absolutely terrify the bear; he went crashing away like a thunderbolt.

May 14, 1958: I have finally begun hunting in the more open woodland adjacent to the dark pine forest, but even here I have met only with frustration. I have roused out nothing but rabbits, and these I am totally unable to catch—lunge after them as I will! They are too small, and I lose sight of them in the brush. Nevertheless, I thrill to the role of predator!

May 17, 1958: O God—it has happened—as I feared it would, as I knew it would! Yesterday—a dark, overcast day, threatening rain—I was prowling in a small birch wood quite some distance from the deep pine forest. A fringe of this birch wood, a thin finger of trees, thrusts out almost to the edge of a dirt road which skirts the area. To amuse myself I crept through this fringe of trees, keeping well hidden, and peered down into the road. A scant ten yards up this sparsely-traveled trace, an old woman hurried along, carrying a sack of something. She kept glancing up at the sky, as if fearing she might get caught in the rain.

My eyes fastened on her, and a trembling seized my whole body. As I stared at her, she looked once over her shoulder, nervously, and hustled on. I can say honestly, in my own defense, that at first I meant only to frighten her. I swear it! As she came abreast, I deliberately cracked some dry twigs on which my palms were resting, and I began to growl. She looked toward the trees, startled, and as I went on growling—louder—she was seized with fear. She dropped the sack and began to run. A red mist seemed to move before my eyes. With no conscious volition of my own I burst out of the trees on all fours, leaped into the road, and bounded after her. She turned once, and terror changed her face to gray putty. Paralyzed with fright, she stood motionless, her mouth open, unable even to scream.

With one flying lunge I crashed upon her, bearing her to earth. An instant later my teeth had fastened in her throat. I bit savagely. Blood spurted into my face. I can remember little more. The blood drove me into an absolute frenzy. I was aware of a vicious snarling, snapping sound which seemed to have its source in the air around me. I can scarcely believe it came from my own throat. Finally the red mist dissolved.

Masked with blood, I found myself crouching on all fours over the body of the old woman. Her head had been very nearly severed. Her face was so slashed and torn that she was unrecognizable.

Slipping into the birch wood, I sought out a nearby pool where I washed the blood from my face. Keeping to the brush and fields, I made my way back to Hemlock House, burned my clothes and collapsed in bed. I lay for hours in a state of exhaustion, with scarcely the energy to move a limb. I was utterly drained of all emotions and impulses. I felt no remorse, no horror—nothing at all.

Only now, as I write these words, can I see the hideous business in its proper perspective. I must either confess to the authorities—or destroy myself.

May 19, 1958: This morning I drove into Juniper Hill. The natives still look stricken when mention is made of the old woman—Alberta Bates. I expressed sympathy. Not a shred of suspicion attaches to me.

They are blaming some wild beast of the forest. Some mention a bear—I reported having seen one—others a wolf. Last winter, they tell me, was unusually severe. It is believed that starving wolves may have come down from Canada and that some are still here. Well, now the idiot yokels have something to talk about. The tedium of their days has at last been interrupted! I feel absolutely secure. The road, though dirt, was so hard-packed that no tracks of any kind could be found. They tried dogs on the trail but got nowhere because a heavy rain had set in several hours before anyone found the poor old woman's body.

I have decided neither to surrender nor to destroy myself. After all, it was not even murder, in the truest sense. There was really no premeditation. It was done on impulse, a horrible but an unthinking, unplanned act. My own destruction could be of no help to the old woman now.

I shall stay out of the woods and the whole business will soon be forgotten. I must remain calm and dispassionate.

May 25, 1958: I have been out again, running on all fours, but I have become wary now. I remain in the darkest part of the pine forest. Local hunting parties are still out, scouring the woods for the "beast" which killed poor old Alberta Bates. I wish them luck!

May 26, 1958: This morning a group of hunters called, asking permission to conduct a search on my own premises. Of course I consented eagerly. I chuckled to myself as I watched them trudge away through the rain.

June 3, 1958: The hunters have given up. Since Alberta Bates had no relatives, she will not long be missed. I am aware of a sense of *accomplishment* because I have outwitted the village idiots.

June 10, 1958: I must leave Hemlock House at once. This area of dark woods and dismal deserted pasturelands has exerted a malign influence on me—an influence so powerful I cannot combat it. Last night—God help me!—I killed again.

I had been restless all day, but I managed to control my impulses. With the coming of night, however, and the appearance of a great full moon, the tensions tearing at my nerves became too strong to resist. I decided, finally, that I would merely take a walk along the lonely dirt road which skirts much of my own property. I can say in all honesty that was my only intention. I reasoned that the night air and exercise would gradually dissipate the inward fretfulness which I felt was reaching a dangerous stage.

It was a beautiful night. The road was silver-gray under the moon. Everything seemed touched with a soft radiance. It was a landscape of lovely lethal dreams. I became aware of a growing excitement. I kept turning to look up at the moon.

Even then nothing might have happened had not the derelict, Freddy Camberwell, come stumbling into sight. Freddy is the village drunk, a chronically besotted but good-natured fool who sleeps in farmers' barns and occasionally does odd jobs for drink money.

He came reeling along, talking to himself, singing snatches of song. There was no thinking, no deliberation, on my part. The chance meeting seemed predestined, fixed inexorably by that strange silver moon.

Dropping to all fours, I raced up the road, straight toward him.

He didn't see me till I was scant yards away. He

stared, rubbed his eyes, not sure whether I was real or only a phantom born of the bottle. An instant before I sprang, his eyes widened and he opened his blubbery mouth to scream. Then he was down on the road, and I was tearing at his throat. His scream came out like a rabbit's bleat. The red mist moved over my eyes; there was a humming sound in my ears and a mad, deep-throated growling which I seemed to be hearing from a far distance.

Later—seconds, minutes, I have no idea—the mist cleared, and I found myself hunched there in the silver moonlight, drenched with blood—but calm, so wonderfully, peacefully calm! I glanced at the thing beneath me without interest. He was even more horribly torn than the old woman, but I had no doubt the overpowering reek of alcohol would identify him quickly enough.

No one else had moved into sight on the road. Dodging quickly into the brush, I came cross-lots back toward Hemlock House. On the way I waded for yards along a small stream, pausing long enough to plunge my head into the water and rinse off most of the blood. After tying my clothes into a small bundle which I buried in the garden, I went to bed and slept without waking for nearly ten hours.

June 12, 1958: Juniper Hill has become an armed camp; hunting parties are ranging the hills all over the township. As I expected, the blundering dogs soon lost the trail. They got as far as the stream and then simply milled about in confusion. The body was not found till mid-morning, and by then the trail was pretty cold in any case. Sheriff Macelin called to warn me that "the thing" might be hiding somewhere in my own woods. I have promised to stay in or to venture out only with a loaded shotgun.

Of course I would be a fool to leave Hemlock House now. Suspicion would attach itself to me immediately. I must remain for a time; there can be no alternative.

June 14, 1958: It is going hard on the black bears. They have already killed three. I feel a sense of remorse about this. Generally speaking, they are such comical, good-natured beasts.

June 16, 1958: If anyone ever reads this—God forbid!—I suppose they will expect a report on the growth of long hair on my legs, a sudden increase in the length of my canine teeth, etc. All this of course is only nonsense dreamed up by hack fictioneers —melodramatic trappings, nothing more. But I am convinced that werewolves like myself have existed for centuries. Harassed peasants may have invented the trappings, but I can clearly see now that there is a solid basis in fact for the many legends which have come down through the ages. There must have been many like me. External trappings invented for effect are nothing compared to the hidden horrors which exist in unseen convolutions of our brains—brains subjected to who knows what monstrous pressures, derangements, diseases, hereditary taints!

June 18, 1958: I am staying close to Hemlock House. It is not safe yet to venture into the woods. The villagers have now killed seven stray dogs, a bobcat, a large gray fox—and two more bears. Not one *wolf* has been seen!

June 22, 1958: Yesterday the mail brought Sabine Baring-Gould's volume, *The Book of Were-Wolves: Being an Account of a Terrible Superstition.* I had ordered the book some days ago. It was published in London in 1865 by Smith, Elder and Co. It must be quite scarce; I had to pay $25 for this copy in poor condition. The volume is a mine of fascinating information. The author writes in his preface, "When a form of superstition is prevalent everywhere, and in all ages, it must rest upon a foundation of fact . . ." True! True! I have no doubt my own case will be preserved in the legends of lycanthropy. This diary I bequeath to posterity!

June 25, 1958: The madness is clawing within me again, shredding my nerves! I no longer feel remorse. In any case the two I have killed were nonentities of importance to no one except themselves.

June 26, 1958: If only those fools from Juniper Hill would stop roaming the woods! But I think their hunter's fever is finally abating. They, too, have a blood thirst. They have killed at least twenty blameless animals. I must admit this nags at my conscience a bit. These local hunters are worse than I! I killed only when a form of madness overcame me. They kill in cold blood!

July 1, 1958: I understand that the last "patrols" have come out of the woods. The search for the "thing" has been given up. At last!

July 3, 1958: Today I returned to the pine forest and ran about on all fours. What a feeling of relief, of release, of utter abandonment. The blood hunger is pounding in my veins again, but I must be careful. I must be cunning—cunning as a wolf!

July 10, 1958: I must annihilate myself! I am ruined, utterly and eternally! I have destroyed a young innocent, and I am sick with remorse! But I must put down the facts.

In late afternoon I was roaming the roads not far from the village. As I came around a bend in the road, I noticed a small girl—six or seven years old—walking along, swinging a pail. I imagine she had been picking blueberries near the roadside and was now returning to Juniper Hill. I cannot believe that she had been given permission to go off alone—probably she had disobeyed and stolen away, chuckling to herself as she gleefully filled her little pail with ripe blueberries.

I tried to calm myself. I actually stopped walking, but I began to tremble and I knew—O God—that I was lost! The risk—the proximity of the village —made no difference to me. In the grasp of this hideous impulse, I appear to have no control over my own movements; the higher centers of my brain congeal into insensibility. In seconds I was a ravening beast plunging up the road on all fours, teeth bared for the death strike!

The innocent did not hear me. I leaped upon her and tore out her soft little throat, and she did not even make an outcry. Perhaps she was stunned, even unconscious, after I hurled her to the earth. I fervently hope so. I was still snarling and slashing when, somehow, a sound penetrated the wall of red mist which surrounds me at these times. It was the creak of a farm wagon coming up the road. I had only seconds in which to snatch up the dead girl and leap into the roadside brush. Filled with horror, remorse and frantic fears, I waited while the wagon slowly rattled past. Luckily the driver was looking straight ahead and did not notice the fresh pool of blood on the road.

As soon as he was out of sight, I piled branches and dead leaves over the girl's body and hurried off. I dared not be seen on the roads. I returned in a roundabout way through woods, fields, and swamps. It was an exhausting four-hour ordeal.

July 15, 1958: The body of the little girl, Debra Dorman, was found only a few hours after her death.

A search party noticed blood in the road and quickly located the corpse under the pile of leaves where I had left it. The dogs again proved useless, losing my trail in a swampy tract nearby. But Juniper Hill is now in a dangerous mood.

The morning after my deed of infamy, Sheriff Macelin and some men he had deputized came pounding at my door. At first I had a horrible fear that all was lost, but I soon found that they only wanted me to join one of the search parties hunting for "the monster." Of course I dared not refuse. For the better part of three days and nights I have been member of a group tramping through bog and brush in search of "the mad wolf," "the thing"—or whatever they choose to call it at the moment.

Volunteers have come in from all over the county. Round-the-clock hunts are continuing relentlessly. I was finally relieved only because it was evident that I must either sleep or drop with exhaustion. I have now had fifteen hours of sleep and feel reasonably rested.

But I am still too tired to experience any emotions. I am what I have become. Perhaps it will pass away, existing finally only as an evil memory.

July 17, 1958: The "wolf hunt" goes on, but I think some of the hunters are beset by a growing sense of futility. I joined a party yesterday afternoon for several hours. Although few have voiced the thought, I believe there may be a growing suspicion that the "wolf" may not be an animal after all. I scoffed at this, but one of the search party pointed out that a predatory killer wolf would undoubtedly attack sheep, cows, and goats as well as stray human beings. Of course no slain livestock have been found, and this fact is causing great uneasiness. I should have killed a sheep or two, just for appearance's sake, but I had little desire to slay domesticated animals. Well, it is too late now, in any case.

I must be extremely careful. I recalled with a fear-ful start that Baring-Gould's *Book of Were-Wolves* was lying on the table when Sheriff Macelin and the deputies called. Apparently no one noticed the title of the book.

July 20, 1958: The hunts continue, stubbornly, but no one now believes the killer will be run to earth by routine methods. A desire is stirring within me to slip into the pine woods and run about on all fours, but I dare not. Armed men, never alone, may be en-countered anywhere.

No one ventures outside of the village without a gun. At night the roads are utterly deserted, except for an occasional hunting party.

I must remain in Hemlock House, no matter how fierce the urges which ride me.

July 24, 1958: It is all over! I could stand the in-tolerable tension no longer. A thousand demons seemed to be churning within me, demanding release. At last I succumbed. Even so, I retained enough common sense to realize that I must not roam in the immediate vicinity of Juniper Hill.

About noon I got into my car and drove some forty miles north. About three o'clock I parked by the side of the road and began to walk. The road led past run-down farmlands and patches of dense forest. For miles I saw only two farm houses, one of them deserted and sagging into ruins. I met not a soul. Finally, toward dusk, I came upon a sort of camp site or state park. Here I spotted a car pulled off the dirt road into the deep brush. I immediately surmised that it must contain two lovers.

Getting down on all fours, I edged into the bushes and advanced toward the vehicle with pounding heart! As I arose and peered into the car window, I saw that I was correct. A young man and girl were inside locked in a tight embrace.

The red mist swam before my eyes! Leaping forward, I wrenched open the car door. I cannot remember all the details. I know that the young man tried to fight, but it was useless. When the madness is upon me, my strength and fury match that of any jungle beast! I dragged him out of the car, hurled him to earth and fastened my teeth in his throat. His frenzied struggles were as nothing. I was still tearing and slashing at his throat when I remembered the girl. Lifting my head, I heard screaming and a crashing in the nearby brush. I was after her in an instant, snarling with renewed blood lust!

Just as she reached the road, I sprang upon her. She crumpled in a heap, suddenly mute and motionless with terror. My dripping teeth were only inches from her jugular when lights flashed up the road, and I heard the sound of excited voices.

Bounding away, I raced along the road, intent now only on escape. Behind me I heard a great tumult of shouting and wild commands.

What followed was a nightmare. A dozen times I was forced to lunge off the road and hide in the brush. By sheer luck I reached my car before it had been located. I drove away recklessly, wiping the blood from my face as I went. But as I passed a crossroad, the headlights picked out the shape of a man, a local farmer I presume, walking along. He looked up, startled, and then—damn his yokel soul to eternal torment—glanced at my license plate. If he remembered the numbers, all is over.

The above happened yesterday, and I wrote the account this morning. It is now afternoon. I have barricaded the downstairs doors. I fear the worst. If only I had paused long enough to kill both the girl and that fool farmer. I fear she may be able to describe me and that he will report my license number. Either could ruin me!

I am finished. They must have traced me! A mob is gathering around the house. I can hear crashes as rocks are hurled through windows. Someone is calling for me to surrender. I shall not! That mob will tear me to pieces.

Sheriff Macelin yells up that he will protect me if I surrender. The mob is screaming! I am tempted to rush out and rip a few more throats before I go down.

I cannot breathe! Tear gas is flooding the room! I must—

Note: Through the heroic efforts of Sheriff Macelin and his deputies, the fiend who penned the above was finally rescued from the lynch mob and hurried away to jail in another township. Although the prosecution subsequently made an impassioned demand for the death penalty, the introduction of the monster's diary by the defense left no doubt in the jurors' minds that its author was hopelessly mad. The unspeakable butcher was committed for life to an institution for the criminally insane. God grant that he there remain.

The
Corpse
of
Charlie Rull

Charlie Rull had been dead for three days. He had been crossing through the cattail swamp adjacent to his shack shelter in the city dump when the heart attack struck. Thirty years of cheap whiskey, greasy food and general physical abuse had finally caught up with him. He toppled into a scum-covered pool; there he lay, unmourned and unremembered.

Ordinarily, that would have been the end of it. Someday, of course, a muskrat hunter or another derelict might have run across a skeleton with a few shreds of cloth adhering to its discolored bones. Even that was unlikely; the enormous marsh rats had teeth like steel chisels.

But Charlie Rull's bulky corpse was not doomed to such prosaic oblivion, for Charlie had pitched forward into a pool of such fiery, ferocious energy, the strongest, rawest alcohol he ever drank would have seemed like watered milk beside it.

By day the pool shimmered with its fierce concentrated life; after dark it glowed white, as if a thousand phosphorescent will-o'-the-wisps had suddenly converged.

Two miles away, across the route skirting the swamp, some of the best scientists in the nation were conducting electron experiments of a nature so secret even the plant guards were not allowed inside the main laboratory. The buildings were entirely surrounded by towering steel-mesh fences wired for instant electrical charges. Armed guards maintained a twenty-four hour vigil.

Although nothing could get into the plant laboratories, something did get out; deadly electronic waste. Liquid thimblefuls were carelessly dumped. Only a few drops at a time. But day after day the lethal drops trickled down the laboratory drains. Even then nothing much might happened if the waste had mixed with the city sewage in the big disposal plants and been carried out to sea.

But, unknown to the laboratory maintenance men, a nearby sewage pipe had cracked. Instead of running off into the main sewage system of the city, the deadly drops seeped through the crack into the swamp. Here they entered a sluggish stream which culminated in the pool where Charlie Rull had toppled dead. Drop by drop, the radiant waste collected, until the pool itself seemed alive.

The frogs, the mud turtles, and the snails which originally inhabited the pool had long since died. The first dose of radiation had killed them within hours. Everything else had died also—even the cattails and the algae.

The waste could not kill Charlie Rull because he was already dead when he struck the scummy water. His corpse, blue and bloated, floated head down in the deadly bath. After three days and nights the radiation had permeated every disintegrating cell of his body. His corpse became saturated with it. It might be said that his swollen carcass, dead as it was, became alive with radiation.

And then a very strange and a very terrifying thing happened. It was an event which would have surprised even the scientists in the plant laboratory. Eventually, perhaps, they could have explained it, but even they would have been incredulous witnesses to the nightmare.

Although the radiation had swiftly killed the frogs, the turtles, and snails, it had had an opposite effect on the corpse of the alcoholic derelict, Charlie Rull. The fierce, fearfully concentrated pool of radiation surrounding the cadaver of the hobo finally penetrated and saturated every atom of it. Radiation, instead of oxygen, quickened the ruined brain cells. Radiation energized the shredded nerve ends, pulsed through the slack sinews.

The corpse of Charlie Rull began to vibrate in the pool as if a giant fish had hold of it. At length it began to twist and writhe. If it felt anything, it must have been in agony. At first it clawed downward toward the mud. Finally it spun over on its back and threshed to the surface. For just a second it floated motionless, its bulging white eyes staring straight up.

Then it started to kick and lunge. By design or accident it attained the edge of the pool and jerked forward through the dead cattail stalks.

When it reached relatively solid ground, it paused as if uncertain how to navigate. After scrambling forward a few feet on its knees and elbows, it stopped again, hesitating. Then it stood on its hands and began to walk, its glassy-eyed head reared up out of the grass like that of a monstrous snake. Eventually it lost balance and toppled over. But soon it rose again, and this time it found its feet.

With this improved form of navigation, its energy, its strength, and what might be called its purpose intensified. Basically, it possessed no human hungers or desires; it did not even retain memory.

But it had one fearful, fixed compulsion. That compulsion was to rid itself of the tremendous dose of radiant energy which coursed and ripped through its fibers like white-hot flame. And the only way to discharge that energy was to exert it, to expend it.

Shambling swiftly through the swamp grass, it approached the nearby parkway. At intervals it stopped, ripped up great tufts of grass by the roots and slammed them back to earth. Once it tore up a small maple tree, bent it double, and hurled it yards away.

Stopping at the edge of the highway, it thrust its bloated fish-belly face through the brush and surveyed the road with fixed filmy eyes which did not even appear to see. Then it slid down the embankment onto the macadam.

At that particular time of morning the parkway was not heavily traveled. The first car, isolated from any others, came along at a good clip, rounded a curve and headed straight toward what appeared to be a drunken tramp, careening along in the middle of the road.

Although the driver slammed on his brake and hit the horn, the crazy hobo did not even attempt to leap aside. The car slowed, but not nearly enough; it rammed into the derelict, knocking him down. When the car finally came to a stop, the tramp was out of sight underneath.

Cursing, the salesman driver shot a quick glance at his rearview mirror, saw that there was no one behind him, and decided to keep on going. Why get into a peck of trouble over a drunken derelict who was actually far more at fault than he himself?

But the car did not respond when the salesman pressed the accelerator. Something seemed to be holding it back. The driver stuck his head out of the window just as the rear end of the car rose into the air. A second later it flipped over, landing on the highway upside down.

Miraculously, the driver was not hurt. His first thought was that he had struck some freak circus strong man out on a drunken spree. A moment later, ultimate terror ended all coherent thought.

The puffy, gray-white face which appeared at the window was that of a corpse which had been long immersed in water. Its glazed, out-of-focus eyes were the eyes of a corpse. And yet it seemed to shine and pulsate with a kind of inward energy.

When it reached through the window with its long hairy arm, the driver was already half-dead with fright, unable to move. The thing's claw-like fingers, armed with heavy black nails, closed over his face and tore the flesh away from his cheek bone. He screamed in agony. Then it seized him by the throat and dragged him toward the window. His head came out but the rest of him, sprawled awkwardly inside the overturned car, stuck.

The thing grabbed him by the head with both huge hands and began to pull and twist in a kind of maniacal fury. His shrill screams quickly turned to strangled gurgles.

When the thing finally got him through the window, his head was attached by little more than a shred of muscle and bone. In a matter of minutes his body was no longer recognizable. The thing tore it to pieces. Then it repeatedly lifted up the car and slammed it down in the highway. At length, after the wreck burst into flames, it moved away.

A few yards further along, a big brown rabbit dashed into the road, stopped squarely in the center and inquisitively eyed the approaching pedestrian.

In life, the tramp would have looked on the rabbit as a potential ingredient for that evening's mulligan stew. An attempt would have been made to catch it for culinary purposes. In death, all this was forgotten. Whatever residual impulses remained in the derelict's wrecked brain cells were impulses only of viciousness and hatred. The negative emotions which had smoldered throughout a lifetime of frustration and bitterness now flickered crazily and uncontrollably in the artificially stimulated cerebral structure.

The rabbit lived; it looked healthy and happy. Therefore, it was an object which aroused instant hatred and fury. It must be caught and crushed to death. Also, some of this horror's searing, unbearable energy might be consumed in the process of destruction.

With a great leap, the thing lunged toward the rabbit. For a second the small animal froze in terror; then it shot off the highway into the adjacent swamp area, escaping capture by inches.

The thing hurtled after it, ploughing through vines, weeds, and clumps of cattails. At one point the maniacal pursuer nearly caught the trembling beast. Shortly afterward however, the hunter lost it in the brush tangle. Trampling and flailing its arms in berserk fury, it continued along the fringe of the swamp not far from the highway.

Meanwhile, a number of cars had passed and seen nothing—nothing, that is, until they came upon the burning wreck and the hideously rent corpse of the unlucky driver. A few who were not too ill to resume driving, rushed off to report the ghastly find.

The thing sloshed through the swamp border for nearly a mile before it again emerged onto the highway. It had forgotten the rabbit but it was still consumed by lethal savagery and by a ferocious impulse to expend the monstrous energy which pulsated inside it like streaking fire.

At this point it saw the hitchhiker.

He was lounging along the edge of the road, rather perfunctorily extending a thumb toward whatever traffic appeared. An olive-skinned young man, sporting a neat toothbrush moustache, he was the picture of vagabond Latin insouciance. His flashing black eyes and brilliant smile were a temptation to most of the lady motorists. Of course they had no way of knowing about the switchblade and the length of strong cord artfully concealed in the young man's pockets.

The hitchhiker was startled, but not frightened, by the appearance of the derelict who shambled out of the weeds alongside the road.

Shrewdly inspecting the newcomer, the young man concluded the tramp was reeling away from an all-night "alki" session in the nearby hobo jungle. The bum might be mean, but he looked too drunk to be dangerous.

The hitchhiker was flip. "Hi, sport. Looks like you really tied one on!"

The tramp did not reply. His red-rimmed, fish-belly eyes regarded the young man with a baleful stare. Disregarding the possibility of oncoming traffic, he lunged across the road.

The hitchhiker jumped aside, scrambled halfway up the highway embankment and whipped out his switchblade.

He, too, was a killer. But he preferred to kill quietly in the darkness while his female victims lay securely bound and gagged.

Nevertheless, he was not as yet unduly alarmed. The bum was crazy drunk, but he didn't seem to have any weapon, and he looked clumsy.

The sight of the switchblade did not stop the derelict. He began climbing the embankment, awkwardly but swiftly.

There was something about the tramp's swollen, death-like face, something about his glazed bulging eyes, which the young man found unaccountably disconcerting. But he suppressed an impulse to run and instead slashed forward and down with the switchblade.

He was quick as a cobra. The razor-sharp blade sliced through the puffy flesh of the vagrant's face. The hitchhiker struck again; the blade slashed alongside the drunk's head, nearly severing an ear.

The hitchhiker then leaped quickly backward, ready to cut again if need be. He assumed that the bum, punished as he was, would back off down the embankment. In this he was mistaken. In spite of his wounds, the derelict kept coming.

Just before the tramp sprang toward him, the young man noticed something which drained him of every last drop of what might charitably be called courage. Although his attacker had been slashed twice, severely, in the face and alongside the head, not a drop of blood flowed out of the cuts. The left ear itself dangled upside down, bloodless.

With a wild yell of terror, the hitchhiker dropped his knife, spun about, and sprinted toward an open field which extended along the embankment.

The tramp bounded after him.

The field was separated from the top of the embankment by a low stone wall. In his frantic haste to scramble over the wall, the hitchhiker did not see the single strand of barbed wire which had been stretched just above the stones of the wall as a deterrent to trespassers. Catching his foot on the wire, he fell headlong.

Before he could gain his feet, the drunken tramp had pounced on him. Galvanized by ultimate terror, he struggled frenziedly. But he was doomed. He was in the grip of a thing which possessed the strength and ferocity of a great animal, of a maddened gorilla or a tiger driven by fury.

The thing began to tear him apart piecemeal. His shrill tortured screams echoed up and down the highway, across the entire width of the field to the edge of the distant trees.

When the tramp finished, what remained in his hands resembled something fresh out of a butcher's shop. He turned, shambled back to the edge of the embankment and hurled the red bundle down onto the highway.

Something swinging against his face irritated him. Reaching up, he wrenched off his dangling left ear and tossed it down after the shapeless remains of the hitchhiker.

Then he climbed over the wall and started across the field.

Little three-year-old Cynthia was playing in the big meadow back of her house when she glanced up and saw the bogeyman. He was hiding in the trees at the edge of the meadow, watching her.

She ran screaming toward the house, her chubby legs churning, her blonde head seeming to bounce among the buttercups and daisies.

Hearing her frightened cries, Mrs. Mellett met her at the back door. She assumed the little one had seen a snake, a toad, or some such creature.

Cynthia rushed into her arms, sobbing with fear. "Mommy! Mommy! Bogeyman! Bogeyman!"

Puzzled, Mrs. Mellett gazed across the meadow. It looked empty. A barn swallow skimmed over the wild flower tufts and that was all.

As she watched, frowning, something lurched out of the trees at the edge of the meadow. It was a man, streaked with blood, advancing swiftly in a grotesque sort of shambling run.

The thing had been watching little Cynthia for some time. It had been puzzled. Her small blond head, barely level with the tops of the buttercups, had seemed to be something growing in the field like a big yellow flower. But suddenly the big flower had darted away, making noises, and now the thing finally realized that it was something alive which might be torn apart.

Leaping into the meadow, it lunged after the little one.

Mrs. Mellett's first impulse was to hurry forth and meet the man. He looked as if he had been severely injured; he would need help.

But something made her hesitate. Some obscure prompting of fear, whose source she could not have named, held her in the doorway, clutching the child.

The thing was nearly across the meadow before she

got a clear look at it. Its bloated, blood-splattered face was gray and shapeless like that of a dead man; its filmy cataleptic eyes did not resemble those of a sentient human being. One ear was missing. The thing's clothes were torn, wet and filthy, crusted with what appeared to be dried blood.

It saw them both now and rushed through the meadow's last fringe of grass and flowers.

Mrs. Mellett wavered no longer. Snatching up little Cynthia, she sprang inside, slammed and bolted the door.

Reaching the door, the thing scrabbled at it briefly and then hurled itself against the panels.

Guided by an instinct beyond her knowledge, Mrs. Mellett had already hurried through the house. As the splintering crash of wooden panels reached her ears, she slipped quickly through the front door, closed it as soundlessly as possible, and cradling Cynthia in her arms, hurried toward an adjacent hay field on the opposite side of the house, where the tall grass afforded cover.

She was gambling that the tramp would first search the house. Yet she was afraid to go far for fear the intruder might see her through the windows and rush out. As soon as possible she stretched prone in the deep grass of the field. Whimpering, Cynthia crouched beside her.

It sounded as if a cyclone were tearing at the house. She could hear the rending of wood, the crash of glass, the heavy thump as plaster struck the floor. For nearly half an hour the roar of destruction continued, seeming to advance from room to room, from floor to floor.

At length the racket ceased. Mrs. Mellett was sure the invader had finally come out of the wrecked house. She hugged the earth, praying, pressing her hand over little Cynthia's mouth to stifle the sound of her whimpering.

For a minute or two there was silence. Then Mrs.

Mellett heard the horse in the nearby corral neighing nervously. In a moment she heard its flying hooves, heard its shrill trumpeting of terror.

The hooves raced around and around, furiously, frantically. Abruptly they stopped, and the horse screamed.

Mrs. Mellett thought she was going to faint; she had never heard a horse scream before.

Clutching little Cynthia, she lay in the tall grass weak with fright for nearly an hour.

At last she dared look up. There was no one in sight. Inch by inch she moved out of the field toward the path which led to the highway. Cynthia huddled in her arms, tear-stained, but now too tired to cry.

She got into the path which passed the corral. She didn't want to look toward the enclosure, but felt she must. She decided not looking might be worse.

When she saw what the thing had done to the horse, she did faint.

After ripping the horse apart, the blood-spattered corpse of Charlie Rull wandered back into the meadow where it had noticed little Cynthia. She was not to be found in the house; possibly, therefore, she was back where she had first been seen.

Not locating her, the thing lost interest in the Mellett farm and wandered back into the woods. Occasionally it seized one of the smaller trees and either tore it up by the roots or broke it in two.

Coming out of the woods farther along, it entered another field. Here, either because of an aimless impulse or because of a retrogressive tendency of its ruined brain cells, it decided to crawl.

It was crawling along the edge of the field, like a great truncated serpent, when it saw the culvert. Perhaps because it was already dead, the dark round hole intrigued it. At any rate it entered the culvert and crawled through.

The culvert led under the highway to the borders of

the cattail swamp adjacent to the city dump. Soon the thing was crawling through the cattails in an area which had been previously familiar to it. Because it began to sink and flounder in the scum-covered pools of this swamp strip, it rose and walked on its feet again, just as if it were alive.

The three tramps were warming up a tin can full of mulligan stew when they heard a crackling in the nearby bushes.

Grumbling, one of them stirred the coals of their rank camp fire. "I bet that's Crazy Zack come for supper. Never brings a scrap, but 'e spots a cook fire a mile away!"

Another spat into the surrounding darkness. "He can sit and watch. He ain't gettin' my share."

All three of them looked up as the bushes parted and someone stepped into the outer fringe of feeble firelight.

The uninvited supper guest looked strangely white. He seemed to shimmer and glow as if his entire body and clothes were coated with some kind of phosphorescent powder.

The tramp who had spoken first scowled into the shadows. "That you, Zack? What makes you shine like that?"

Instead of replying, the newcomer lurched swiftly toward the fire.

Instinctively, the three of them leaped up and spread apart.

With an expression of awed recognition, one of the tramps exclaimed: "It's Charlie Rull! Hurt! Hurt real bad!"

Charlie Rull swung his head to survey the speaker with malignant, fish-belly eyes in which there was no faint glimmer of recognition.

The tramp backed off, trembling. "Now Charlie, I ain't never crossed you. 'Member the pint we split, last New Year's? 'Member—"

...arlie, apparently, remembered nothing. His ... lips twisted in a snarl of fury as he sprang forward.

The tramp whirled to run, but Charlie Rull, terribly injured as he appeared to be, was too fast. His great hands fastened on his ex-drinking partner like the claws of some raging beast of prey gone mad with rabies or pain. The terrible, taloned hands, glowing with white fire, began to rip the flesh from the bones as if it were loose, wet putty.

The blood-chilling shrieks of the victim rang in the ears of the other two derelicts as they shot off through the cattails. They were hardened hoboes to whom brutality was a way of life, yet they pressed their hands over their ears as they careened away crazily through the underbrush.

At last the thing desisted. Staring down at the red stump which it held in its hands, it hurled it away into the darkness.

Then it noticed the fire. Here in the darkness the fire appeared to be something alive. The thing seized it, but the little red dancers broke away and fell on the ground.

In a renewed burst of fury, the thing kicked savagely at the red dancers, scattering them in all directions.

They disappeared briefly, but then they started dancing in the darkness again. The more they danced the bigger they got, and finally they were dancing all around the dead thing. Some dim, vestigial apperception told the corpse of Charlie Rull that the red dancers could not be grasped and torn apart.

As he pushed through them, they seized the shredded remains of his clothes and danced all over him. He felt little or nothing, but he struck at them because they irritated and confused him. At length they dropped away and he headed back the way he had come, toward the highway.

By the time he reached it, the cattail swamp behind him was a roaring wall of flame.

Terrified parkway drivers, sick with horror, had long since notified the police of nearby Newbridge of what might be found out on the road skirting the city dump. And then Mrs. Mellett, weak with shock, had stumbled into a neighboring farmhouse and gasped out an incredible story.

At first the police had been skeptical. But their skepticism vanished when they saw the shredded, mutilated remains on the highway. And an examination of the Mellett house added to their apprehension. The inside of the house was a shambles —gutted as thoroughly as if a tornado had whirled within. The dismembered carcass of the horse, scarcely more than a series of red smears scattered around the corral, added further confirmation.

Both ends of the highway which extended alongside the dump and the adjacent swamp area were shut off by roadblocks, manned by police armed with high-powered rifles. At one end a machine gun was set in readiness. Helicopters were sent up in the hopes that they might be able to locate the lethal thing of madness which lurked in the vicinity.

Residents of suburban Newbridge were warned to remain in their houses behind locked doors. Fearfully, the citizens of the entire city huddled by their television and radio sets, listening to the frequent reports sent out by the newscasters and police who were guarding the roadblocks.

As darkness descended, a report came in that the swamp near the highway had caught fire. Hurrying to their windows, people saw a red glare reflected on the sky. It seemed like a macabre stage prop set up for the thing from Hell which had suddenly appeared in their midst.

The helicopters came in as night settled down.

They had seen nothing except streaking tongues of fire in the burning cattail marsh.

Searchlights were turned on at the roadblocks. The police checked their rifles and waited.

The thing appeared without warning. A reporter noticed something white and shining veer onto the highway. A moment after he had alerted the police guard, the white shape shambled into the search-light's glare.

A collective murmur of incredulity and revulsion arose. The nightmarish, blood-drenched thing which stumbled into the light resembled a disinterred corpse. Most of its clothes had been ripped or burned away. It had only one ear. Its glazed, baleful eyes stared out of a bloated face which might have been painted by Goya.

A hellish halo surrounded it, as if every cell was suffused and alive with radium.

For a moment it blinked in the sudden light. Then a snarl of fury twisted its mottled, puffy face. Awkwardly, but with unexpected and terrifying speed, it rushed toward the roadblock.

The police captain in charge of the roadblock had time only for the single command: "Fire!"

The crash of rifles broke the night. The thing spun around, staggered backward and then, although half of its face appeared to be shot away, leaped forward again.

The police captain touched the shoulder of the sergeant crouched behind the machine gun. A staccato chatter mingled with the heavier crash of rifle fire.

The first concentrated burst cut the thing in two. The upper torso fell forward completely detached from the lower trunk and legs.

And then a thing happened which made the police guards freeze with horror, even though most of them were war veterans to whom carnage was not unknown. Two of the reporters fainted on the spot.

Detached as it was, the severed upper torso began to hitch itself along the highway on its hands, the glare of hatred in its eyes entirely undimmed. The legs, attached to the lower trunk, toppled onto the road, yet they continued to scrape forward like some giant, scissoring, two-legged crab.

The police captain, the brittle edge of near-hysteria changing his voice, swore at his men. "Keep firing, you fools! Keep firing! Did I tell you to stop? Finish it! Finish it!"

Once more heavy rifle slugs lashed into the advancing twin horrors. The machine gun resumed its deadly chatter.

The thing's head spun off. One arm was ripped away. The scrabbling legs threshed crazily as rifle fire all but tore them apart.

At length the indescribable glowing remains could only twist and hitch in aimless circles on the highway. Fierce radiation kept them moving, but merely as detached helpless fragments. A hand, severed by machine-gun fire, crawled sideways off the highway into a ditch. The inhuman glare in the fish-belly eyes gradually faded away.

When the police captain finally gave the order to stop firing, the scattered radiant remnants of the thing had almost ceased to move. For a little while longer some of them continued to twitch and jerk.

Eventually all motion ended. The tortured, shredded corpse of Charlie Rull at last lay still.

Canavan's
Back Yard

I first met Canavan over twenty years ago shortly after he had emigrated from London. He was an antiquarian and a lover of old books; so he quite naturally set up shop as a second-hand book dealer after he settled in New Haven.

Since his small capital didn't permit him to rent premises in the center of the city, he rented combined business and living quarters in an isolated old house near the outskirts of town. The section was sparsely settled, but since a good percentage of Canavan's business was transacted by mail, it didn't particularly matter.

Quite often, after a morning spent at my typewriter, I walked out to Canavan's shop and spent most of the afternoon browsing among his old books. I found it a great pleasure, especially because Canavan never resorted to high-pressure methods to make a sale. He was aware of my precarious financial situation; he never frowned if I walked away empty-handed.

In fact, he seemed to welcome me for my company alone. Only a few book buyers called at his place with regularity, and I think he was often lonely. Sometimes when business was slow, he would brew a pot of English tea and the two of us would sit for hours, drinking tea and talking about books.

Canavan even looked like an antiquarian book dealer—or the popular caricature of one. He was small of frame, somewhat stoop-shouldered, and his blue eyes peered out from behind archaic spectacles with steel rims and square-cut lenses.

Althought I doubt if his yearly income ever matched that of a good paperhanger, he managed to "get by" and he was content. Content, that is, until he began noticing his back yard.

Behind the ramshackle old house in which he lived and ran his shop, stretched a long, desolate yard overgrown with brambles and high brindle-colored grass. Several decayed apple trees, jagged and black with rot, added to the scene's dismal aspect. The broken wooden fences on both sides of the yard were all but swallowed up by the tangle of coarse grass. They appeared to be literally sinking into the ground. Altogether, the yard presented an unusually depressing picture, and I often wondered why Canavan didn't clean it up. But it was none of my business; I never mentioned it.

One afternoon when I visited the shop, Canavan was not in the front display room, so I walked down a narrow corridor to a rear storeroom where he sometimes worked, packing and unpacking book shipments. When I entered the storeroom, Canavan was standing at the window, looking out at the back yard.

I started to speak and then for some reason didn't. I think what stopped me was the look on Canavan's face. He was gazing out at the yard with a peculiar intense expression, as if he were completely absorbed by something he saw there. Varying, conflicting emotions showed on his strained features. He seemed both fascinated and fearful, attracted and repelled. When he finally noticed me, he almost jumped. He stared at me for a moment as if I were a total stranger.

Then his old easy smile came back, and his blue eyes twinkled behind the square spectacles. He shook his head. "That back yard of mine sure looks funny sometimes. You look at it long enough, you think it runs for miles!"

That was all he said at the time, and I soon forgot about it. I didn't know that was just the beginning of the horrible business.

After that, whenever I visited the shop, I found Canavan in the rear storeroom. Once in a while he was actually working, but most of the time he was simply standing at the window looking out at that dreary yard of his.

Sometimes he would stand there for minutes completely oblivious to my presence. Whatever he saw appeared to rivet his entire attention. His countenance at these times showed an expression of fright mingled with a queer kind of pleasurable expectancy. Usually it was necessary for me to cough loudly or shuffle my feet before he turned from the window.

Afterward, when he talked about books, he would seem to be his old self again, but I began to experience the disconcerting feeling that he was merely acting, that while he chatted about incunabula, his thoughts were actually still dwelling on that infernal back yard.

Several times I thought of questioning him about the yard, but whenever words were on the tip of my tongue, I was stopped by a sense of embarrassment. How can one admonish a man for looking out of a window at his own back yard? What does one say and how does one say it?

I kept silent. Later I regretted it bitterly.

Canavan's business, never really flourishing, began to diminish. Worse than that, he appeared to be failing physically. He grew more stooped and gaunt. Though his eyes never lost their sharp glint, I began to believe it was more the glitter of fever than the twinkle of healthy enthusiasm which animated them.

One afternoon when I entered the shop, Canavan was nowhere to be found. Thinking he might be just outside the back door engaged in some household chore, I leaned up against the rear window and looked out.

I didn't see Canavan, but as I gazed out over the yard I was swept with a sudden inexplicable sense of desolation which seemed to roll over me like the wave of an icy sea. My initial impulse was to pull away from the window, but something held me. As I stared out over that miserable tangle of briars and brindle grass, I experienced what for want of a better word I can only call *curiosity*. Perhaps some cool, analytical, dispassionate part of my brain simply wanted to discover what had caused my sudden feeling of acute depression. Or possibly some feature of that wretched vista attracted me on a subconscious level which I had never permitted to crowd up into my sane and waking hours.

In any case, I remained at the window. The long dry brown grass wavered slightly in the wind. The rotted black trees reared motionless. Not a single bird, not even a butterfly, hovered over that bleak expanse. There was nothing to be seen except the stalks of long brindle grass, the decayed trees, and scattered clumps of low-growing, briars.

Yet there was something about that particular isolated slice of landscape which I found intriguing. I think I had the feeling that it presented some kind of puzzle, and that if I gazed at it long enough, the puzzle would resolve itself.

After I had stood looking out at it for a few minutes, I experienced the odd sensation that its perspective was subtly altering. Neither the grass nor the trees changed, and yet the yard itself seemed to expand its dimensions. At first I merely reflected that the yard was actually much longer than I had previously believed. Then I had an idea that in reality it stretched for several acres. Finally, I became convinced that it continued for an interminable distance and that, if I entered it, I might walk for miles and miles before I came to the end.

I was seized by a sudden almost overpowering desire to rush out the back door, plunge into that sea of wavering brindle grass, and stride straight ahead until I had discovered for myself just how far it did extend. I was, in fact, on the point of doing so—when I saw Canavan.

He appeared abruptly out of the tangle of tall grass at the near end of the yard. For at least a minute he seemed to be completely lost. He looked at the back of his own house as if he had never in his life seen it before. He was disheveled and obviously excited. Briars clung to his trousers and jacket, and pieces of grass were stuck in the hooks of his old-fashioned shoes. His eyes roved around wildly; he seemed about to turn and bolt back into the tangle from which he had just emerged.

I rapped loudly on the window pane. He paused in a half turn, looked over his shoulder, and saw me. Gradually an expression of normality returned to his agitated features. Walking in a weary slouch, he approached the house. I hurried to the door and let him in. He went straight to the front display room and sank down in a chair.

He looked up when I followed him into the room. "Frank," he said in a half whisper, "would you make some tea?"

I brewed tea, and he drank it scalding hot without

saying a word. He looked utterly exhausted; I knew he was too tired to tell me what had happened.

"You had better stay indoors for a few days," I said as I left.

He nodded weakly, without looking up, and bade me good day.

When I returned to the shop the next afternoon, he appeared rested and refreshed but nevertheless moody and depressed. He made no mention of the previous day's episode. For a week or so it seemed as if he might forget about the yard.

But one day when I went into the shop, he was standing at the rear window, and I could see that he tore himself away only with the greatest reluctance. After that, the pattern began repeating itself with regularity. I knew that that weird tangle of brindle grass behind his house was becoming an obsession.

Because I feared for his business as well as for his fragile health, I finally remonstrated with him. I pointed out that he was losing customers; he had not issued a book catalogue in months. I told him that the time spent in gazing at that witch's half acre he called his back yard would be better spent in listing his books and filling his orders. I assured him that an obsession such as his was sure to undermine his health. And finally I pointed out the absurd and ridiculous aspects of the affair. If people knew he spent hours in staring out of his window at nothing more than a miniature jungle of grass and briars, they might think he was actually mad.

I ended by boldly asking him exactly what he had experienced that afternoon when I had seen him come out of the grass with a lost bewildered expression on his face.

He removed his square spectacles with a sigh. "Frank," he said, "I know you mean well. But there's something about that back yard—some secret—that I've got to find out. I don't know what it is exactly—something about distance and dimensions and perspectives, I think. But whatever it is, I've come to consider it—well, a challenge. I've got to get to the root of it. If you think I'm crazy, I'm sorry. But I'll have no rest until I solve the riddle of that piece of ground."

He replaced his spectacles with a frown. "That afternoon," he went on, "when you were standing at the window, I had a strange and frightening experience out there. I had been watching at the window, and finally I felt myself drawn irresistibly outside. I plunged into the grass with a feeling of exhilaration, of adventure, of expectancy. As I advanced into the yard, my sense of elation quickly changed to a mood of black depression. I turned around, intending to come right out—but I couldn't. You won't believe this, I know—but I was lost! I simply lost all sense of direction and couldn't decide which way to turn. That grass is taller than it looks! When you get into it, you can't see anything beyond it."

"I know this sounds incredible—but I wandered out there for an hour. The yard seemed fantastically large—it almost seemed to alter its dimensions as I moved, so that a large expanse of it lay always in front of me. I must have walked in circles. I swear I trudged miles!"

He shook his head. "You don't have to believe me. I don't expect you to. But that's what happened. When I finally found my way out, it was by the sheerest accident. And the strangest part of it is that once I got out, I felt suddenly terrified without the tall grass all around me and I wanted to rush back in again! This in spite of the ghastly sense of desolation which the place aroused in me.

"But I've got to go back. I've got to figure the thing out. There's something out there that defies the laws of earthly nature as we know them. I mean to find out what it is. I think I have a plan and I mean to put it into practice.''

His words stirred me strangely and when I uneasily recalled my own experience at the window that afternoon, I found it difficult to dismiss his story as sheer nonsense. I did—half-heartedly—try to dissuade him from entering the yard again, but I knew even as I spoke that I was wasting my breath.

I left the shop that afternoon with a feeling of oppression and foreboding which nothing could remove.

When I called several days later, my worst fears were realized—Canavan was missing. The front door of the shop was unlatched as usual, but Canavan was not in the house. I looked in every room. Finally, with a feeling of infinite dread, I opened the back door and looked out toward the yard.

The long stalks of brown grass slid against each other in the slight breeze with dry sibilant whispers. The dead trees reared black and motionless. Although it was late summer, I could hear neither the chirp of a bird nor the chirr of a single insect. The yard itself seemed to be listening.

Feeling something against my foot, I glanced down and saw a thick twine stretching from inside the door, across the scant cleared space immediately adjacent to the house and thence into the wavering wall of grass. Instantly I recalled Canavan's mention of a "plan." His plan, I realized immediately, was to enter the yard trailing a stout cord behind him. No matter how he twisted and turned, he must have reasoned, he could always find his way out by following back along the cord.

It seemed like a workable scheme, so I felt relieved. Probably Canavan was still in the yard. I decided I would wait for him to come out. Perhaps if he were permitted to roam around in the yard long enough, without interruption, the place would lose its evil fascination for him, and he would forget about it.

I went back into the shop and browsed among the books. At the end of an hour I became uneasy again. I wondered how long Canavan had been in the yard. When I began reflecting on the old man's uncertain health, I felt a sense of responsibility.

I finally returned to the back door, saw that he was nowhere in sight, and called out his name. I experienced the disquieting sensation that my shout carried no further than the very edge of that whispering fringe of grass. It was as if the sound had been smothered, deadened, nullified as soon as the vibrations of it reached the border of that overgrown yard.

I called again and again, but there was no reply. At length I decided to go in after him. I would follow along the cord, I thought, and I would be sure to locate him. I told myself that the thick grass undoubtedly did stifle my shout and possibly, in any case, Canavan might be growing slightly deaf.

Just inside the door, the cord was tied securely around the leg of a heavy table. Taking hold of the twine, I crossed the cleared area back of the house and slipped into the rustling expanse of grass.

The going was easy at first, and I made good progress. As I advanced, however, the grass stems became thicker, and grew closer together, and I was forced to shove my way through them.

When I was no more than a few yards inside the tangle, I was overwhelmed with the same bottomless sense of desolation which I had experienced before. There was certainly something uncanny about the place. I felt as if I had suddenly veered into another world—a world of briars and brindle grass whose ceaseless half-heard whisperings were somehow alive with evil.

As I pushed along, the cord abruptly came to an end. Glancing down, I saw that it had caught against a thorn bush, abraded itself, and had subsequently broken. Although I bent down and poked in the area for several minutes, I was unable to locate the piece from which it had parted. Probably Canavan was unaware that the cord had broken and was now pulling it along with him.

I straightened up, cupped my hands to my mouth, and shouted. My shout seemed to be all but drowned in my throat by that dismal wall of grass. I felt as if I were down at the bottom of a well, shouting up.

Frowning with growing uneasiness, I tramped ahead. The grass stalks kept getting thicker and tougher, and at length I needed both hands to propel myself through the matted growth.

I began to sweat profusely; my head started to ache, and I imagined that my vision was beginning to blur. I felt the same tense, almost unbearable oppression which one experiences on a stifling summer's day when a storm is brewing and the atmosphere is charged with static electricity.

Also, I realized with a slight qualm of fear that I had got turned around and didn't know which part of the yard I was in. During an objective half-minute in which I reflected that I was actually worried about getting lost in someone's back yard, I almost laughed—almost. But there was something about the place which didn't permit laughter. I plodded ahead with a sober face.

Presently I began to feel that I was not alone. I had a sudden hair-raising conviction that someone—or something—was creeping along in the grass behind me. I cannot say with certainty that I heard anything, although I may have, but all at once I was firmly convinced that some creature was crawling or wriggling a short distance to the rear.

I felt that I was being watched and that the watcher was wholly malignant.

For a wild instant I considered headlong flight.

Then, unaccountably, rage took possession of me. I was suddenly furious with Canavan, furious with the yard, furious with myself. All my pent-up tension exploded in a gust of rage which swept away fear. Now, I vowed, I would get to the root of the weird business. I would be tormented and frustrated by it no longer.

I whirled without warning and lunged into the grass where I believed my stealthy pursuer might be hiding.

I stopped abruptly; my savage anger melted into inexpressible horror.

In the faint but brassy sunlight which filtered down through the towering stalks, Canavan crouched on all fours like a beast about to spring. His glasses were gone, his clothes were in shreds and his mouth was twisted into an insane grimace, half smirk, half snarl.

I stood petrified, staring at him. His eyes, queerly out of focus, glared at me with concentrated hatred and without any glimmer of recognition. His gray hair was matted with grass and small sticks; his entire body, in fact, including the tattered remains of his clothing, was covered with them as if he had grovelled or rolled on the ground like a wild animal.

After the first throat-freezing shock, I finally found my tongue.

"Canavan!" I screamed at him. "Canavan, for God's sake don't you know me?"

His answer was a low throaty snarl. His lips twisted back from his yellowish teeth, and his crouching body tensed for a spring.

Pure terror took possession of me. I leaped aside and flung myself into that infernal wall of grass an instant before he lunged.

The intensity of my terror must have given me added strength. I rammed headlong through those twisted stalks which before I had laboriously pulled aside. I could hear the grass and briar brushes crashing behind me, and I knew that I was running for my life.

I pounded on as in a nightmare. Grass stalks snapped against my face like whips, and thorns gashed me like razors, but I felt nothing. All my physical and mental resources were concentrated in one frenzied resolve: I must get out of that devil's field of grass and away from the monstrous thing which followed swiftly in my wake.

My breath began coming in great shuddering sobs. My legs felt weak and I seemed to be looking through spinning saucers of light. But I ran on.

The thing behind me was gaining. I could hear it growling, and I could feel it lunge against the earth only inches behind my flying feet. And all the time I had the maddening conviction that I was actually running in circles.

At last, when I felt that I must surely collapse in another second, I plunged through a final brindle thicket into the open sunlight. Ahead of me lay the cleared area at the rear of Canavan's shop. Just beyond was the house itself.

Gasping and fighting for breath, I dragged myself toward the door. For no reason that I could explain, then or afterwards, I felt absolutely certain that the horror at my heels would not venture into the open area. I didn't even turn around to make sure.

Inside the house I fell weakly into a chair. My strained breathing slowly returned to normal, but my mind remained caught up in a whirlwind of sheer horror and hideous conjecture.

Canavan, I realized, had gone completely mad. Some ghastly shock had turned him into a ravening bestial lunatic thirsting to savagely destroy any living thing that crossed his path. Remembering the oddly-focused eyes which had glared at me with a glaze of animal ferocity, I knew that his mind had not been merely unhinged—it was totally gone. Death could be the only possible release.

But Canavan was still at least the shell of a human being, and he had been my friend. I could not take the law into my own hands.

With many misgivings I called the police and an ambulance.

What followed was more madness, plus a session of questions and demands which left me in a state of near nervous collapse.

A half dozen burly policemen spent the better part of an hour tramping through that wavering brindle grass without locating any trace of Canavan. They came out cursing, rubbing their eyes and shaking their heads. They were flushed, furious—and ill at ease. They announced that they had seen nothing and heard nothing except some sneaking dog which stayed always out of sight and growled at them at intervals.

When they mentioned the growling dog, I opened my mouth to speak, but thought better of it and said nothing. They were already regarding me with open suspicion as if they believed my own mind might be breaking.

I repeated my story at least twenty times, and still they were not satisfied. They ransacked the entire house. They inspected Canavan's files. They even removed some loose boards in one of the rooms and searched underneath.

At length they grudgingly concluded that Canavan had suffered total loss of memory after experiencing some kind of shock and that he had wandered off the premises in a state of amnesia shortly after I had encountered him in the yard. My own description of his appearance and actions they discounted as lurid exaggeration. After warning me that I would probably be questioned further and that my own premises might be inspected, they reluctantly permitted me to leave.

Their subsequent searches and investigations revealed nothing new and Canavan was put down as a missing person, probably afflicted with acute amnesia.

But I was not satisfied, and I could not rest.

Six months of patient, painstaking, tedious research in the files and stacks of the local university library finally yielded something which I do not offer as an explanation, nor even as a definite clue, but only as a fantastic near-impossibility which I ask no one to believe.

One afternoon, after my extended research over a period of months had produced nothing of significance, the Keeper of Rare Books at the library triumphantly bore to my study niche a tiny, crumbling pamphlet which had been printed in New Haven in 1695. It mentioned no author and carried the stark title, *Deathe of Goodie Larkins, Witche.*

Several years before, it revealed, an ancient crone, one Goodie Larkins, had been accused by neighbors of turning a missing child into a wild dog. The Salem madness was raging at the time, and Goodie Larkins had been summarily condemned to death. Instead of being burned, she had been driven into a marsh deep in the woods where seven savage dogs, starved for a fortnight, had been turned loose on her trail. Apparently her accusers felt that this was a touch of truly poetic justice.

As the ravening dogs closed in on her, she was heard by her retreating neighbors to utter a frightful curse:

"Let this lande I fall upon lye alle the way to Hell!" she had screamed. *"And they who tarry here be as these beastes that rende me dead!"*

A subsequent inspection of old maps and land deeds satisfied me that the marsh in which Goodie Larkins was torn to pieces by the dogs after uttering her awful curse—originally occupied the same lot or square which now enclosed Canavan's hellish back yard!

I say no more. I returned only once to that devilish spot. It was a cold desolate autumn day, and a keening wind rattled the brindle stalks. I cannot say what urged me back to that unholy area; perhaps it was some lingering feeling of loyalty toward the Canavan I had known. Perhaps it was even some last shred of hope. But as soon as I entered the cleared area behind Canavan's boarded-up house, I knew I had made a mistake.

As I stared at the stiff waving grass, the bare trees and the black ragged briars, I felt as if I, in turn, were being watched. I felt as if something alien and wholly evil were observing me, and though I was terrified, I experienced a perverse, insane impulse to rush headlong into that whispering expanse. Again I imagined I saw that monstrous landscape subtly alter its dimensions and perspective until I was staring at a stretch of blowing brindle grass and rotted trees which ran for miles. Something urged me to enter, to lose myself in the lovely grass, to roll and grovel at its roots, to rip off the foolish encumbrances of cloth which covered me and run howling and ravenous, on and on, on and on. . . .

Instead, I turned and rushed away. I ran through the windy autumn streets like a madman. I lurched into my rooms and bolted the door.

I have never gone back since. And I never shall.

The
Pavilion

During the summer months the beach pavilion swarmed with people. Crowds sauntered up and down its front boardwalk, darted in and out of the little enclosed dressing rooms which ran along on piles nearly the length of a city block, and in general infested every square foot of the immense structure.

But during the cold months the huge building, as well as the beach adjacent to it, was totally deserted. Icy winter winds from the open sea moaned through its darkened interior. Sometimes big waves flung themselves across the boardwalk and swirled around the base of the piles. Only a few front locker rooms were equipped with electricity, but during the summer, brilliant sun usually penetrated the slat roof, creating a clear but subdued light which was entirely pleasant and adequate. During the overcast days of winter, however, very little light came through the roof. The inside of the pavilion became full of shadows, cold, damp and gloomy—the last place in the world where any sane person would want to go.

Niles Glendon was the exception. As he started out for the pavilion one cold, cloudy afternoon in late February, he was entirely sane. He had a reason for going.

He had paid a visit to the pavilion some four months before under rather unusual circumstances. Then he had driven to the pavilion with his old friend Kurt Resinger. Kurt, however, hadn't had much choice in the matter. During the drive to the beach, he had lain huddled on the floor in the rear of Niles' car, limp and purple-faced, with Niles' finger marks still on his squeezed gullet.

Kurt had been foolish enough to refuse Niles a small loan of five hundred dollars. Little enough, Niles figured, after all the favors Kurt had accepted in the past. Little enough after the dozens of times Niles had gotten him out of jams. When Niles ran into a flurry of bad luck, instead of coming to his aid, Kurt had grown distant. And that day in late October had been the finish.

Kurt had finally reluctantly agreed to meet Niles at a crossroads not too far from the beach which was a convenient halfway point for both of them. Once there however, he had flatly refused Niles' request for a loan and had finally intimated that so far as he was concerned their friendship was at an end.

Niles, white with fury, had controlled himself with effort. And then, when they were parting, Kurt's car had refused to start. Masking his violent anger, Niles had offered to drive Kurt home. Once away from the crossroads, out on the deserted beach highway, Niles had repeated his request for a loan. Again Kurt refused, and this time Niles' fury had exploded savagely. Braking the car to a sudden stop, he had whirled, seized Kurt by his thin throat, and mercilessly throttled the life out of him.

After appropriating Kurt's wallet, which contained

a helpful eighty dollars, he had jammed the corpse out of sight on the floor of the car and driven to the beach pavilion. It was a chill, rainy day in late October and the big building had been deserted. Nobody had been in sight along the beach. Fetching a small shovel from his car, Niles had dragged the corpse of his old friend into the pavilion and buried it in the sand among the piles. When summer came, he knew, people would be hurrying about on the plank walks only six or seven feet overhead, but he had little fear that the body would be discovered. Who would ever want to climb down from the plank walks and start digging in the damp sand at the base of the piles?

During the ensuing winter however several fierce storms had raged along the beach. Niles had read newspaper accounts which stated that huge waves had washed inland, creating damage to shore properties. Undoubtedly, he reflected, a large amount of sea water had flooded in under the boardwalks of the beach pavilion, surging and swishing among the piles. It was possible that some of the sand had been swept about. It was even possible that his old friend Kurt had been disturbed in his rude resting place. . . .

As he drove toward the beach this dreary afternoon in late February, he was not really worried. In the first place, he was under no suspicion. He had been questioned after Kurt's disappearance, as had all Kurt's other friends, but the grilling had been a mild one, a mere routine. No one had seen him at the crossroads meeting and no one had seen him near the beach. After a thorough investigation, the police began to lean toward the suicide theory, and of course, in many subtle ways, Niles fostered the idea.

Beyond that, even if his old friend's sandy grave *had* been disturbed by the winter storms, Niles felt that he could repair the damage easily enough.

Nobody would stop at the pavilion till at least April. Certainly he was unlikely to encounter anyone on a raw, windy day in February.

He drove down the beach road without passing a single car, and when he pulled up near the pavilion, not a living soul was in sight.

As he climbed out of the car and started walking toward the beach, he was surprised at the force of the wind. It was a damp, penetrating wind which struck through his clothes and made him shiver.

Under a dark sky, the beach was a spectacle of desolation. For as far as the eye could see, great gray waves pounded far up on the empty sands. A litter of rubbery green seaweed twitched and tossed at the tideline.

As Niles stood watching, a single sea gull swung down out of the overcast and scrutinized him sharply with its cruel eye. He considered that an evil omen. Shivering, he walked toward the pavilion.

As he moved along the outside boardwalk, he noticed that many of the wooden slats had been torn up by the wind and waves. Some were holding by a nail or two and others were strewn about loose. He entered the shadowy building with reluctance, his feet echoing hollowly on the plank walks.

As he advanced into the darkened interior, he began to wish he had not come. It seemed colder, damper, and drearier inside than out. It occurred to him that the entire building at this time of the year resembled nothing so much as a huge tomb.

Glancing nervously at the creaking, half-open doors of the little dressing rooms as he passed along, he was startled enough to freeze in his tracks as he suddenly saw a pair of sneakers protruding from under one cubicle. The shoes were empty of course, abandoned by some hurried or forgetful swimmer the summer before, and he felt angry with himself for his foolish fright.

He went on, further and further into the immense building, and soon he saw with misgivings that a number of the inside plank walks had collapsed. That probably meant that the wind-driven waves had very definitely gotten inside.

Peering over the frail hand railing, he stared down at the sunken piles which supported the building. They appeared secure enough, but he noticed that the bed of sand was damp and riddled by puddles. Also, the sandy floor was no longer smooth and even. In some spots the sand had been heaped up in little mounds; in others it had been scooped out, leaving hollows.

Definitely worried now, Niles hurried out of the building and returned to the car for his shovel, cursing himself for not having brought it in the first place. As he strode back along the beach, half running, spray from the big, incoming waves slapped against his face. Swearing, he wiped his sleeve against his cheek.

Back inside, he looked around to get his bearings. There were five parallel plank walls running the length of the pavilion. When he buried his old friend Kurt, he had been careful to note the exact location—just in case. Kurt was lying in the sand near the base of the eleventh pile running along the second plank walk from the left as one faced the rear of the building.

Congratulating himself on his foresight in memorizing the specific location, he crossed to the second plank walk and hurried along until he reached the eleventh pile. Then he swung under the hand railing and dropped to the damp sand below.

It seemed colder than ever down under the boardwalks. It was so cold he didn't mind the exertion of digging. He was probably being foolish, he told himself, since the sand at this particular spot didn't appear to have been greatly disturbed by the invading winter waves. Just to feel secure in his own mind, however, he would dig until he struck the corpse. Once he was positive it had not been dislodged, he would refill the hole, pound the sand down hard with his shovel and depart.

He dug energetically and in no time at all was two feet down. The wet sand yielded easily under his shovel. Another foot or so and the shovel should strike something which would offer more resistance.

Confidently he dug another foot. He began to handle the shovel gingerly, waiting for it to thump against the grisly remainder which he knew was there. But the thump never came. Sea water began seeping slowly into the hole, and that was all.

Perspiring, he leaned against the pile and stared down into the dark hole. Perhaps, he told himself, the corpse had settled further into the wet sand during the winter months. Its own weight had forced it downward; the loose sand had yielded under the pressure and now the corpse lay inches further down than it had when first buried. Yes, that must be the answer.

Reassuring himself, he began to dig again. But after he had dug down another foot, he uncovered nothing but more sand, and now water began welling rapidly into the hole. He climbed out with a hollow, sick feeling in the pit of his stomach and looked around rather wildly. If the corpse wasn't where he had buried it, *where was it*? He could understand that the waves might have washed away some of the sand, but it hardly seemed likely that they could have completely disinterred the cadaver. *Or could they?*

Taking a firm grip on the shovel, he began prowling about under the piles. In the gray light, he could see only a few yards ahead. He walked in a half crouch, peering to left and right. Once he whirled around with a pounding heart as he heard a noise somewhere behind him. It was a sagging plank bumping against the top of one of the piles.

After he had prowled for ten minutes and found nothing, he began to think that he had made a mistake. Perhaps it had been the *third* walk from the left instead of the second, or possibly it was the *tenth* pile instead of the eleventh.

Well, it was worth a try. Since it was obvious that he would have been more apt to miscount the piles rather than the walks, he returned under the second plank aisleway and started digging at the base of the tenth pile.

He dug four feet straight down and struck nothing. Trembling, he climbed out of the watery hole and stared around with a sense of growing panic. Either he had made a very great mistake in memorizing the location of the cadaver or else. . . .

With a supreme effort of will he controlled his rising hysteria and systematically refilled the two holes he had already dug. He would try digging alongside the eleventh pile in the *third* walk, he told himself. Quite possibly, in the gloom of the pavilion that previous October, he had counted three aisles as two.

He dug again, and again his shovel revealed nothing save seeping sea water. As he finally stopped digging and squirmed out of the briny pit, perspiring and panting, a new, fantastic and utterly gruesome thought struck him and he was touched by genuine terror. Was it *possible* that his old friend Kurt had not been quite dead when Niles buried him in the wet sand that day? Had the cold and the dampness revived him? Had he perhaps clawed his way upward out of the sand? Persons trapped in such situations were known to possess the sudden strength of madmen. And the sand was not like hard-packed earth; it was loose, light. . . .

Frenzied with horror at this thought, Niles began racing up and down between the rows of piles. With his terror, paradoxically enough, came insane rage. He began screaming the name of his old friend, cursing him, daring him to show himself.

As he lunged up and down and in and out among the piles, a rising wind whipped through the pavilion, slamming the little dressing-room doors, rattling the railings, howling shrilly under the roof. Also, the sea waves, flung at the crest of a rising tide, began swirling over the outer boardwalks.

In a few minutes the damp sand floor of the pavilion started covering with water as the wind-driven tide beat shoreward with increasing strength.

Niles, sloshing in water up around his ankles, scarcely noticed. He darted about in the semi-darkness under the walks like some monstrous ferret on the trail of an elusive hare. He bolted about like a maniac, slashing at shadows with his shovel, glaring between the piles as if he saw enemies closing on all sides of him.

"You're hiding, damn you!" he screamed. "I know you're here! I'll find your filthy carcass! I know you're here! *I know you're here!*"

As he bolted and raged about, bereft of reason, the incoming tide rose to his knees and began creeping higher. He paused finally, weak with exhaustion, and leaned against a pile.

It was then that he saw it. It came floating placidly out of the farthest dark corner of the pavilion, there where the supporting piles were grouped so closely together it was almost impossible to see. Propelled by the tide, it glided toward him unhurriedly, face up and grinning, faintly phosphorescent, its fish-belly eyes rolled so far back in its head only the whites remained visible.

Minutes before he had been ready to rend and smash it with his shovel. Now that he saw it in actuality, swirling toward him with its half-fleshed face and its hideous lipless grin, sheer, heart-squeezing terror crowded out every other emotion. His only impulse was to escape.

While a hoarse scream of madness wrenched itself from his throat, he leaped upward wildly and clutched at the overhead boardwalk. Missing, he fell backward with a great splash, jamming his leg between two adjacent piles. As he struck the water, he twisted violently and the combined pull and impact broke his shin bone. It cracked audibly. The white-hot pain was so intense, it cut through even his terror. He screamed underwater, and his mouth immediately filled with brine.

Thrashing about like a harpooned fish in the shallows, he finally got his head above water. The pain in his leg was indescribable, but as the first blinding shock of it was over, he comprehended the full horror of his situation.

He was unable to move without screaming, and the water was now rising rapidly. And that ghastly grinning thing with its flat white eyes began floating toward him again.

As it approached, full terror took possession of him. Momentarily he forgot the fierce pain in his leg, forgot the water that was inching upward all about him. His only thought was to avoid having the horror touch him.

When it was inches away, he lurched violently. The movement jammed his broken leg tighter between the piles and hurled him down and backward as if he had been struck with a pile driver.

He plunged under water, half unconscious with pain and terror, overwhelmed with sudden weakness. By the time he realized he was drowning, he could not make it back up. Once he almost got his face above the water, but his strength failed and he fell backward. For a few seconds he twisted and turned under the water. At length a tiny trail of bubbles swirled upward and disappeared.

As the tide continued to rise however, it accomplished what his fatal upward lunge had not been able to do. It lifted his fractured leg between the piles and gently floated him free—even as it had floated free the storm-disinterred corpse of Kurt Resinger, stuck between piles in the far corner.

Darkness came on; the wind moaned; the tide rose even higher. Round and about among the piles, swirling and gliding, went two grotesque shapes, two old friends, bobbing and nodding together at the bottom of the tomb-black pavilion.

House
of Memory

Tara had the happiest childhood of anyone I've ever known. The big white Sutter house on Maple Street seemed to spill over with happiness. With its smooth front lawn and enormous back yard it was a mecca for the neighborhood children. In the spring the gleaming white house seemed enveloped in a drifting cloud of apple blossoms. In autumn, surrounded by scarlet maples, it remained a shining white attraction.

Tara loved the place, loved every individual tree and bush—you might almost say every blade of grass. The word is much abused, but I think you could call her childhood idyllic. Her worst experience was a broken arm, but right after she broke it, Aunt Millie came down from Boston and stayed a whole month. With Aunt Millie around, who could fret about a broken arm? Not Tara, certainly; Aunt Millie made everything fun. You laughed all day and went to bed laughing.

The golden years went on and it seemed they would go on forever. Tara left for college, but the big white house on Maple Street was still the center of her universe. She'd been out of college about a year and was working in nearby Western Ridge when real tragedy struck.

It was found that her father had cancer. It progressed slowly but relentlessly, and while the doctors fought it with every weapon they possessed, the Sutter money ebbed away. By the time Joel Sutter died, the big white house on Maple Street was heavily mortgaged. After other debts were added up, there was no alternative but to sell.

Tara had borne up well during her father's slow and agonizing decline, but the loss of her childhood home left her heartbroken. When the remaining Sutters moved to a small house on Elwood Street, she actually became ill.

She got better, of course, and life went on, but the white house on Maple Street with its attendant memories was enshrined in her heart and mind.

Less than two years after the move to Elwood Street, the new owner of the Maple Street house died, leaving his estate to a large, quarrelsome, and rather greedy family. Over the years, as Tara's father had slowly declined, the big white house had been badly neglected. Now the new heirs decided the land was worth more than the house, and it would be foolish, they agreed, to spend several thousand dollars on repairs. They therefore had the house torn down and prepared to sell the land.

The news was a shock to Tara, but this time she didn't get sick. Instead she developed "the obsession." It was the only abnormal thing about an otherwise lovable and eminently sensible young lady.

Tara decided that so far as she herself was concerned, the big white house had never been demolished. After the wreckers moved in, she carefully avoided Maple Street. If she happened to be riding home with friends who inadvertently drove down Maple Street, she would turn her head away or even shut her eyes until they were well past the site where the beloved house had once stood. On no occasion did she so much as glimpse the gaping cellar hole. Tight-lipped, she refused to discuss the matter. The house was still there, she insisted, and she wouldn't talk about it.

The family who had razed the house planned to sell the property as a supermarket site, but before the sale went through, they began to quarrel among themselves about the price. The quarrel turned into a bitter family feud. No one would budge. The land remained unsold, and weeds began growing in the old cellar hole.

This new development made no apparent difference to Tara. Whether an empty cellar hole or a supermarket actually occupied the old site, in her own mind the house was still there.

It was about this time that the Sutters—Tara had two sisters and a grown brother, besides her mother—decided to hold a small house party. As a family friend of long standing, I was invited.

Other guests included Aunt Millie, ancient but still irrepressible, Melissa Mowerly, for whom I had a secret "crush," Eric Sanderson, who grew up next door to the Sutters, Jim Clote, Dora Frazier, Frank Yarmon, Pearl Johnson, Ursula Wood, and Mr. Bodmore who had known Aunt Millie for a good many years.

Of course I accepted. I never missed a chance to see Melissa and, like everyone else, I adored Tara.

A few days before the scheduled party, Tara came down with a cold. It got steadily worse and she went to bed with a high fever. Naturally Mrs. Sutter wanted to call off the party, but Tara wouldn't hear of it.

"They've all made plans!" she told her mother. "At least they can stand in the doorway and talk to me. I'll feel a lot worse if they *don't* come!''

Mrs. Sutter sighed and knew she was defeated. Understanding Tara as well as she did, she realized that Tara probably *would* get worse if the party were cancelled. She'd fret and brood and wouldn't be able to sleep. So the party stayed on schedule.

Shortly after we were all assembled at the Sutter house, everyone trooped upstairs to greet Tara. She was sitting up in bed, perfectly ravishing in a beribboned, apricot-colored nightgown and bed jacket. Her face was quite flushed, but I couldn't decide whether her high color was caused by fever or by laughing at Aunt Millie's uproarious remarks.

We crowded in the doorway and assured her that she was just antisocial at heart and wanted Aunt Millie all to herself. She replied gaily, and the banter might have gone on for an hour had not Mrs. Sutter tactfully but firmly intervened.

We went downstairs in high good humor. Every half hour or so Aunt Millie went up to see Tara—against Mrs. Sutter's orders—and shortly afterward we would hear Tara's infectious laughter ring out.

We ate and drank and danced and talked till well after midnight. Mrs. Sutter told us that Tara had finally fallen asleep and that her cough seemed to be better.

The Sutter house was not large and sleeping arrangements were a trifle complicated. I was assigned a cot in a tiny room adjacent to the rear pantry, but it was comfortable enough. Most of the male guests were on the first floor or in the basement; the women found beds upstairs or in the small finished loft.

I had been in bed about an hour and was just falling asleep when some kind of commotion made me sit up. I heard Mrs. Sutter's voice, shrill and agitated, and then a great slamming of doors. I dressed quickly, not knowing what to expect.

I was putting on my jacket when Melissa Mowerly plunged through the door. She was breathless. "Kirk!" she gasped, "you've got to help us! Tara is gone!"

"Gone!" I echoed incredulously.

She nodded. "Mrs. Sutter thinks she woke up with a fever and went outside. But we can't find her. She may have fallen somewhere!"

I grabbed her arm. "Let's go!"

Mrs. Sutter and someone with a flashlight were already outside near the front porch. Melissa and I moved toward the back, calling, "Tara! Tara! Tara!" loudly, wildly.

As we skirted the shrubbery more lights went on inside the house.

We peered into the half darkness, and I glanced up at the cold October moon. "Did Tara have anything on besides a nightgown?"

Melissa shrugged. "The closet door was open. Mrs. Sutter thinks she may have taken a coat or a jacket or something, but we didn't take time to check through all her clothes."

I suddenly had a hunch. "Come on!" I said. Holding Melissa's hand, I started to run through the big back yard toward the rear gate which led into Summer Street.

As the gate clashed shut behind us and we started down the street, Melissa suddenly stopped. "Kirk, I don't think she would get far. Where are we going?"

"Maple Street," I answered. "Hurry!"

Maple Street was only about seven blocks from Summer and we reached it in record time, considering the circumstances. Panting, we finally paused as we turned into the street.

A pattern of moonlight and shadow, blurred somehow by a sheen of accumulating frost, did tricks with one's vision. At first I saw only an empty street crisscrossed by tree shadows. Then, far down on one side, I glimpsed a small hurrying figure.

"There she is!" I told Melissa, and we both started to run again.

We were about halfway down Maple Street when the figure before us turned in off the sidewalk. I realized at once that she had reached the approximate site of the old Sutter house, the big white house of her happy, vanished childhood.

I sprinted forward. I didn't want her to fall into that old cellar hole, didn't want her to—

Within a few yards of the spot where she had turned in, I suddenly stopped in absolute amazement, paralyzed and speechless.

It was Tara all right, wearing slippers and some kind of short jacket over her nightgown. She was going up the flagged path from the sidewalk—but she wasn't going up toward a gaping, empty cellar hole.

Striding swiftly, she was approaching a big white house aglow with lights, standing sharp and clear in the frosty moonlight.

As I watched, frozen with disbelief and a terror which made my heart pound, she reached the porch. She was about to start up the porch steps when I finally found my voice.

"Tara!"

She stopped, reluctantly it seemed, and very slowly turned around.

I can't recall precisely what emotion possessed me at that moment. It was primarily, I guess, fear—fear of the unknown, fear for Tara, and a conviction for which I actually had no real grounds: Tara must at all costs be called back from that visible and yet impossible house which loomed before me in the moonlight. "Tara! Don't move! Don't move! Wait for me!" I rushed up the path.

I caught her just as she swayed and pitched forward. Momentarily my attention was diverted from everything else. After I had got a firm grip on her and saw that she had apparently fainted, I glanced up.

I was standing on the edge of a black and empty cellar hole. There was no house, no sign of any house.

I looked around wildly. Melissa, ashen-faced, was still standing on the sidewalk.

"You saw it too?" I asked in a hoarse voice. "You saw the white house?"

She nodded mutely, unable to speak.

For days Tara hung between life and death. She had not merely fainted when I caught her, but had lapsed into a comatose state brought on by raging fever. Very slowly she fought her way back to consciousness and life, but many months passed before she recovered fully.

Melissa and I never mentioned the big white house which both of us had seen where actually only an empty cellar hole existed.

Months later, when we were alone together, the subject came up. I knew Melissa had been brooding about it, and now she questioned me.

"Well, you see," I said, "it's simply that Tara had the image of that house so firmly stamped in her own mind, especially that night when she was feverish and probably groping subconsciously toward the past, that she was able, all unknowing of course, to transmit to our own minds an actual visual reproduction of the house."

Melissa frowned. "In other words, all we saw was a picture sort of projected from Tara's own mind, like telepathy." Melissa was not entirely satisfied with my explanation, but she accepted it.

Of course we both wondered whether Tara remembered any part of that impossible night. Naturally, we didn't question her about it. We did notice, however, that she appeared to have lost her "obsession." She no longer closed her eyes or looked away when she was riding down Maple Street. She'd look right at the old cellar hole where the Sutter house had stood.

Then one day she spoke out.

"Remember the night of the party?" she began. "Well, I had the strangest experience. I suppose you'll insist it was just a fever dream, but it was very real to me. Anyway, it seemed I got up out of bed, put on a jacket and walked alone through the night back to Maple Street. And do you know—*there was our old house!* It was exactly as I've always remembered it. All the lights were on and I was just about to start up the porch steps . . . ."

She hestiated and put a hand to her head. "Well, I forget what happened *then*. But I'm convinced that our old house really does still exist."

Mrs. Sutter smiled gently. "But Tara, dear, we passed the cellar hole on Maple Street only yesterday. You saw it."

Tara nodded and frowned. "I know that. I guess what I mean is that the *past* exists—somewhere. The house doesn't actually exist today, but it still exists in yesterday's time. And yesterday's time is forever!"

My eyes met Melissa's. Both of us were remembering a big white house, lights blazing, standing sharp and clear in the frosty moonlight.

The
Willow
Platform

Thirty years ago Juniper Hill was an isolated township with a small village, dirt roads, and high hilly tracts of evergreen forest—pine, hemlock, tamarack, and spruce. Scattered along the fringes of wood were boulder-strewn pastures, hay fields, and glacially-formed, lichen-covered knolls.

Ordinarily I stayed in Juniper Hill from early June until late September. As I returned year after year, I came to be accepted almost as a native—many notches above the few transient "summer people" who stayed for a month or so and then hurried back to the world of traffic, tension, and tedium.

I wrote when I felt like it. The rest of the time I walked the dirt roads, explored the woods, and chatted with the natives.

Within a few years I got to know everyone in town, with the exception of a hermit or two and one irascible landowner who refused to converse even with his own neighbors.

To me, however, a certain Henry Crotell was the

most intriguing person in Juniper Hill. He was sometimes referred to as "the village idiot," "that loafer," "that good-for-nothing," etc., but I came to believe that these epithets arose more from envy than from conviction.

Somehow, Henry managed to subsist and enjoy life without doing any work—or at least hardly any. At a time when this has become a permanent way of life for several million persons, I must quickly add that Henry did not receive one dime from the township of Juniper Hill, either in cash or goods.

He lived in a one-room shack on stony land which nobody claimed, and he fed himself. He fished, hunted, picked berries, and raised a few potatoes among the rocks behind his shack. If his hunting included a bit of poaching, nobody seemed to mind.

Since Henry used neither alcohol nor tobacco, his needs were minimal. Occasionally, if he needed a new shirt or shoes, he would split wood, dig potatoes, or fill in as an extra hay-field hand for a few days. He established a standard charge which never varied: one dollar a day plus meals. He would never accept any more cash. You might prevail upon him to take along a sack of turnips, but if you handed him a dollar and a quarter for the day, he'd smilingly return the quarter.

Henry was in his early thirties, slab-sided, snuff-brown, with a quick loose grin and rather inscrutable, faded blue eyes. His ginger hair was getting a trifle thin. When he smiled, strangers assumed he was wearing false teeth because his own were so white and even. I once asked him how often he brushed his teeth. He doubled up with silent laughter. "Nary brush! Nary toothpaste!" I didn't press the point, but I often wondered what his secret was—if he had one.

Henry should have lived out his quiet days at

Juniper Hill and died at ninety on the cot in his shack. But it was not to be.

Henry found the book.

Four or five miles from Henry's shack lay the crumbling ruins of the old Trobish house. It was little more than a cellar hole filled with rotted boards and fallen beams. Lilac bushes had forced their roots between the old foundation stones; maple saplings filled the dooryard. Old Hannibal Trobish, dead for fifty years, had been an eccentric hermit who drove off intruders with a shotgun. When he died, leaving no heirs and owing ten years' taxes, the town had taken over the property. But the town had no need of it, nor use for it, and so the house had been allowed to decay until finally the whole structure, board by board, had dropped away into the cellar hole. There were hundreds of such collapsed and neglected houses throughout New England. Nobody paid much attention to them.

Henry Crotell, however, seemed fascinated by the mouldering remains of the Trobish house. He prowled the area, poked about in the cellar hole, and even lifted out some of the mildewed beams. Once, reaching in among the sagging foundation stones, he was nearly bitten by a copperhead.

Old Dave Baines admonished Henry when he heard about it. "That's an omen, Henry! You'd better stay away from that cellar hole."

Henry pushed out his upper lip and looked at his shoes. "Ain't 'fraid of no old snake. Seen bigger. Last summer I rec'lect. Big tom rattler twice as big!"

Not long after the copperhead incident, Henry found the book. It was contained in a small battered tin box which was jammed far in between two of the foundation stones in the Trobish cellar.

It was a small, vellum-bound book, measuring about four by six inches. The title page and table of contents page had either disintegrated or been removed, and mold was working on the rest of the pages, but it was still possible to read most of the print—that is, if you knew Latin.

Henry didn't, of course, but, no matter, he was entranced by his find. He carried the book everywhere. Sometimes you'd see him sitting in the spruce woods, frowning over the volume, baffled but still intrigued.

We underestimated Henry. He was determined to read the book. Eventually he prevailed upon Miss Winnis, the local school teacher, to lend him a second-hand Latin grammar and vocabulary.

Since Henry's formal schooling had been limited to two or three years and since his knowledge of English was, at best, rudimentary, it must have been a fearful task for him to tackle Latin.

But he persisted. Whenever he wasn't prowling the woods, fishing, or filling in for an ailing hired hand, he'd sit puzzling over his find. He'd trace out the Latin words with one finger, frown, shake his head, and pick up the textbook. Then, stubbornly, he'd go back to the vellum-bound volume again.

He ran into many snags. Finally he returned to Miss Winnis with a formidable list of words and names which he couldn't find in the grammar.

Miss Winnis did the best she could with the list. Shortly afterwards she went to see Dave Baines. Although, in his later years, Baines held no official position, he was the patriarch of the town. Nearly everyone went to him for counsel and advice.

Not long after Miss Winnis' visit, he stopped in to see me. After sipping a little wine, he came to the point.

"I wish," he said abruptly, "you'd try to get that damned book away from Henry."

I looked up with surprise. "Why should I, Dave? It keeps him amused apparently."

THE WILLOW PLATFORM   71

Baines removed his steel-rimmed spectacles and rubbed his eyes. "That list Henry brought Miss Winnis contains some very strange words—including the names of at least four different devils. And several names which must refer to—entities—maybe worse than devils!"

I poured more wine. "I'll see what I can do. But I really can't imagine what harm could come of it. That book is just a new toy to Henry. He'll tire of it eventually."

Dave replaced his spectacles. "Well, maybe. But the other day Giles Cowdry heard this funny high-pitched voice coming out of the woods. Said it gave him the creeps. He slipped in to investigate, and there was Henry standing in a clearing among the pines reading out of that moldy book. I suppose his Latin pronunciation was pretty terrible, but Giles said a strange feeling came over him as Henry went on reading. He backed away, and I guess he was glad enough to get out of earshot."

I promised Dave I'd see what I could do. About a week later while I was taking a walk through the woods in the vicinity of Henry's shack, I heard a kind of chant emanating from nearby.

Pushing through a stand of pines, I spotted Henry standing in a small open area among the trees. He held a book in one hand and mouthed a kind of gibberish which, to me at least, only faintly resembled Latin.

Unobtrusively, I edged into sight. A fallen branch cracked as I stepped on it, and Henry looked up.

He stopped reading immediately.

I nodded. "Mornin', Henry. Just taking a stroll and I couldn't help hearing you. Must be a mighty interesting little book you've got there. Can I take a look at it?"

Ordinarily, Henry would greet me with an easy

grin. This time he scowled. "Ain't givin' my book to nobody!" he exclaimed, stuffing the volume into a pocket.

I was annoyed, and I suppose I showed it. "I didn't ask to *keep* the book, Henry. I merely wanted to look at it." Actually this wasn't entirely true; I had hoped to persuade him to give me the book.

He shrugged, hesitated and then, turning, started off through the woods. "I got chores. No time for talk," he muttered over his shoulder.

The next day I reported my failure to Dave Baines.

"Too bad," he commented, "but I suppose we'd better just forget about it. If he won't give that infernal book to you, he won't give it to anybody. Let's just hope he loses interest in it after a time."

But Henry didn't lose interest in the vellum-bound book. On the contrary, he developed an obsession about it. He went hunting or fishing only when driven by acute hunger. He neglected his potato patch. His shack, never very sturdy, began to disintegrate.

Less often during the day now, but more often at night, his high-pitched voice would be heard arising from one of the dense groves of pines or hemlocks which bordered the dusty country roads. Scarcely anyone in Juniper Hill knew Latin, but everyone who heard Henry's chant drifting from the dark woods agreed that it was an eerie and disturbing experience. One farmer's wife averred that Henry's nocturnal readings had given her nightmares.

Somebody asked how Henry could see to read in the dark since nobody had ever seen a light in the woods when he chanted the words.

It was, as is said, "a good question." We never found out for sure. It was possible that Henry had finally memorized the contents of the book or part of them. This, however, I personally found difficult to believe.

Henry's explanation, when it came, was even more difficult to accept.

One hot summer morning he turned up at the village general store. He looked emaciated and his clothes were in tatters, but he seemed imbued with a kind of suppressed animation. Perhaps exhilaration might be the better word.

He bought a two-dollar work shirt and three tins of corned beef. He did not appear chagrined that these purchases very obviously emptied his tattered wallet.

Loungers at the store noticed that he was wearing a ring. Some commented on it.

Surprisingly, Henry held it out for inspection. He was visibly proud of it. Everyone agreed later that they had never seen a ring like it before. The band might have been shaped out of silver, but worked into it were tiny veins of blue which appeared to glow faintly. The stone was disappointing: black, flat-cut, and dull in luster.

Unusually voluble, Henry volunteered some information on the stone. "Ain't no good in daylight. Nighttime she comes alive. Throws out light, she do!"

He gathered up his purchases and started for the door. He paused at the threshold, chuckling, and turned his head. "Light a-plenty," he added, " 'nuff light to read by!"

Still chuckling to himself, he walked out into the hot sunlight and off down the road.

The only other information we received about the ring came from Walter Frawley, the town constable, who met Henry in the woods one day. Frawley reported that he had asked Henry where he had acquired the ring.

Henry insisted that he had found it, purely by chance, tangled up among the roots of a huge pine tree which formerly grew near the ruins of the old Trobish house. The great pine had toppled in a severe line storm several years before. Natives estimated the tree was at least a hundred years old.

Nobody could satisfactorily explain how the ring had become entangled in the roots of a century-old pine tree. It was possible, of course, as someone suggested, that old Hannibal Trobish had buried it there many decades ago—either to hide it or to get rid of it.

As the hot summer advanced, Henry went on chanting in the woods at night, giving late travelers ''a case of the nerves'' and causing some of the farm watchdogs to howl dismally.

One day I met Miss Winnis in the village and asked for her opinion of Henry's book, based on the list of words and names which he had brought to her for translation or clarification.

''The book is medieval in origin,'' she told me. ''And I think it was written by someone who pretended to be a wizard or sorcerer. Poor Henry is out there in the woods at night chanting invocations to non-existent devils dreamed up by some medieval charlatan who was quite possibly burned at the stake!''

I frowned. ''Why do you say 'non-existent devils,' Miss Winnis?''

''I don't *believe* in such things,'' she replied a bit stiffly. ''I went to Dave Baines about the book because I thought it was having a bad effect on Henry. Heaven knows I'd be delighted if he learned Latin, but I don't think he's going about it properly. And he's neglecting everything. People tell me his little hut is falling apart and that he doesn't eat properly anymore.''

I thanked her and went my way, even more concerned than I had been before, but totally unable to see how I could help. I felt that Henry still liked me, but I knew his stubbornness was monumental.

Not long after my talk with Miss Winnis, I heard

rumors that Henry was building some kind of stage or platform on a small knoll adjacent to one of the deeper stands of hemlock. The knoll was about a mile from one of the less-traveled country roads. It was quite high, almost level with the tops of the hemlocks. I had been on it a few times and recalled that on a clear day it overlooked a huge expanse of forest and field.

One afternoon when the summer heat had subsided somewhat, I went to have a look at Henry's platform. After nearly becoming lost in the dark hemlock woods, I slipped into the sunlight and climbed the side of the knoll, a small hill made up of glacial stones and gravel.

It was barren except for a few stunted shrubs, ground creepers, and dried lichen patches. Centered on the exact top was a twenty-foot structure built primarily out of willow saplings. A few stakes of heavier wood had been driven in around the base to strengthen the whole. The top of the bizarre lookout tapered to a tiny wooden platform, just large enough for one person. A crude hand ladder had been attached to one side and a kind of rail ran around the perimeter of the platform.

It looked, altogether, shaky and perilous. Henry was no heavyweight, and he would probably survive a twenty-foot drop onto the slippery side of a knoll, but I felt, nevertheless, that he was risking serious injury.

I circled the little structure and sat down nearby for a time, but Henry did not appear. At length, as the afternoon sun beat down on the knoll, I got up and made my way uneventfully through the hemlocks and back to the road.

Dave Baines shook his head when he learned of the willow platform. "That Latin book is drivin' Henry loco. I expect he'll fall off that thing, break a leg, or maybe his spine, and end up in the county hospital."

I suggested condemning the willow tower since it was obviously hazardous and was, moreover, built on land to which Henry had no title.

Dave shrugged. "What good would it do? He'd be madder than a hundred wet hens, and he'd likely just go out and rig up another somewhere else."

I let it go at that. I wasn't a native of the town, and I certainly wasn't going to spearhead any "movement" to demolish Henry's willow platform.

Not long after my talk with Dave, the stories started circulating. At night, it was rumored, Henry's chanting could be heard all over town. It was becoming louder all the time.

Frank Kenmore came in with a story about Henry screeching from the top of the willow tower while it swayed wildly in the wind and "tongues of fire" floated over the hemlock trees.

John Pendle complained that his old mare had bolted and thrown him from his buggy into the ditch one night when Henry started his "crazy yellin'."

Young Charlie Foxmire swore that he had crept through the woods at midnight and seen Henry on his tower "laughin' like a madman and talkin' to somebody in the trees."

I determined to find out for myself what actually was taking place. Late one evening I went out to the front veranda and listened. Sure enough, when the wind was right, I could hear Henry's steady chanting.

I turned off my lights and started out for the willow tower.

It was tough going through the hemlocks, but Henry's high-pitched chant kept me on my course. When I reached the knoll, I circled around until I was directly at Henry's back. I advanced only a few feet up the side of the knoll, crouched down, and then very cautiously lifted my head.

Henry, book in hand, was standing on the tiny

platform. The flimsy structure was swaying slightly in the wind. A bluish glow, whose source I could not at first locate, illuminated the book and part of Henry's face. His chant rose and fell eerily. He kept glancing from the book out over the top of the black hemlock forest, almost as if he were addressing a huge unseen audience which listened among the trees. In spite of the relative warmth of the summer night, I found myself shuddering.

His chant seemed to go on endlessly as he turned the pages of the book. His voice became stronger as he continued. The wind rose and the platform swayed a little more.

I crouched motionless until my muscles ached, but there was no response from the depths of the hemlock woods. I was shocked when I realized that I had been *waiting* for a response!

I saw clearly at last that the strange blue glow emanated from the ring on Henry's finger. I experienced the weird conviction that the glow strengthened as Henry's chant grew stronger.

At length, the tension, plus my uncomfortable crouching, began to tire me. I had intended to stay until Henry finished his nocturnal incantations, but on second thought I decided to leave before he descended. I was convinced that he would be furious if he found me spying on him when he came down.

Moving carefully, I slipped backwards into the trees. A carpet of hemlock needles, inches deep, effectively muffled my footsteps. I groped my way to the road and walked home. I was too exhausted to assess the full implications of what I had seen. In spite of my fatigue, I did not sleep well. Unpleasant dreams, bordering on nightmares, harried me until morning.

I reported to Dave Baines. He appeared deeply concerned.

"Henry's going to destroy himself—or be destroyed by something, if we don't get him away from there."

I nodded. "That's the way I feel—but what can we do?"

Dave began polishing his spectacles. "I'll think of something."

Three days later as I was returning from the village store early one morning, I met Henry. He was shuffling along dispiritedly. I inquired, casually, where he was heading.

He stopped, eyes on the ground, and began kicking at the dirt road with one foot.

"Dave Baines," he told me, "got me on over ta Miller's place. Extry hay hand. Says they be hard up fer help. Wants me to go—sort of a favor to *him*!"

He shook his head and scowled. "Wouldn't go fer nobody else. Nobody! But Dave done me favors. Lots of favors. So I got to go."

"That's fine, Henry!" I said. "You'll be well fed and earn a few dollars! The almanac's predicting a long winter!"

He looked at me scornfully. "Ain't worried about winter. You know what I think?"

"What's that, Henry?"

He hesitated. "Well, I trust Dave, I reckon. But it could be somebody put him to it—so's they could get in my shack and take my book!"

His faded blue eyes took on an unfamiliar glint. He continued before I could comment.

"It won't do nobody no good! Because I got my book right here!" He tapped his overall pocket. "Right here!" he repeated triumphantly.

I assured him that Dave was undoubtedly acting in good faith and that nobody I knew in Juniper Hill would trespass in his absence.

Somewhat mollified, but still dispirited, he shuffled off. I noticed that he was still wearing his unusual ring with the flat black stone.

Kent Miller's place was at the far northern end of Juniper Hill. And Miller possessed several huge hay fields. If I judged correctly, Henry would not be back for several days.

That evening I decided to pay another visit to Henry's willow platform. As I started through the hemlock woods toward the knoll, I felt a bit like an intruder. But then I reminded myself that the knoll did not belong to Henry. And perhaps I might stumble on some clue which would be the key to Henry's obsession.

The thick hemlock woods were like a dark and aromatic tomb. I reached the knoll with a feeling of relief. At least I was in the open; I could see sky and feel a breeze on my face.

As I glanced up at the willow tower, I almost laughed aloud. How absurd it looked! Poorly constructed, fragile, swaying in the slight wind—how foolish I was to have been so impressed by a country loafer's childish obsession!

I scrambled up the shaky ladder nailed to one side of the tower and cautiously edged out onto the flimsy platform. The moon had not yet risen and there was not much to see—the dark continuing mass of hemlocks, a few fireflies and, far off, the twinkling light in a farmhouse window.

I was both relieved and disappointed. I told myself that I was a fool. What *had* I expected to see?

As I was about to start down the ladder, I thought I heard a faint chant somewhere in the deep distance. It was like an echo, almost inaudible—yet I paused with my hand on the platform railing and listened.

As I waited, it grew stronger, but only by a small degree. I looked out over the hemlocks and frowned. The contour of the woods seemed to have changed; the outlines of the trees seemed different.

I strained my eyes into the darkness, unable to

comprehend what I thought I was witnessing. The wind rose, and the chant grew louder.

Henry was returning, I told myself, and I must hurry away before he reached the knoll with his infernal book and the ring that glowed in the dark.

Two things happened then almost simultaneously. As I started to let myself over the side to go down the ladder, I glanced once more toward the black mass of hemlocks. Only they weren't hemlocks. They were immense, towering trees, tropical in outline, which resembled giant ferns against the sky.

And as I stared in amazement and disbelief, a figure faced me on the platform—a figure with distorted features and glittering eyes which looked like an evil caricature of Henry Crotell!

With a rush of horror, I realized that I could see *through* the figure to the night sky beyond.

After several moments of immobility, I went over the side of the platform. I slid partway down the apology for a ladder and fell the rest of the way.

As soon as my feet touched earth, they were racing for the trees. And when I entered them, they were the dark sweet hemlocks which I knew.

I rushed through them, gouging and scratching myself on projecting branches. Henry's chant, somewhat weak but still persistent, followed me.

I could hear it, far off in the night, when I stumbled onto my porch and opened the door.

I sat up for hours drinking coffee and at last fell asleep in my chair. I was slumped there, red-eyed and unshaven, when someone knocked.

I got up with a start, noticing that sunlight was pouring through a nearby window, and opened the door.

Dave Baines looked at me keenly, both abashed and a bit amused. "Sorry I woke you up. I'll come back—"

I shook my head. "No, no! Sit down. You're the very person I want to see!"

He heard me out in silence. After he had polished his glasses for five minutes, he spoke.

"I'm not sure, but I'd be willing to venture the opinion that the figure you saw on that platform was what some folks call an 'astral projection.' Henry's still at the Miller place; I called this morning to find out. One of the field hands came in after midnight and saw him fast asleep—he never would have had time to come down here, rant on that crazy tower of his, and walk back again. Henry, consciously or unconsciously, projected part of himself back here to the knoll. A kind of intense wish fulfillment, I guess. Chances are he doesn't even remember it this morning."

I shook my head in disbelief. "But what did I *hear*?"

Dave replaced his spectacles. "You heard his chanting all right, but not with your ears. You heard it inside your head with your mind only. No reason telepathy, or projection, can't be audible as well as visual. It's all the result of a mind's—or a psyche's—fierce desire to be in another place. The desire is so strong that part of that person—call it 'ectoplasm' or what you will—actually does return."

"But what about the trees?" I interjected. "What made the wood and the hemlocks change? Why did I seem to be looking out over a great forest of tropical fern trees—or whatever they were?"

Dave got up, rather wearily. "That I can't explain, at least not now." He sighed. "I wish the whole business was over with. I just have a feelin' Henry's going to come a cropper."

Henry did "come a cropper" the very next night. Just before dusk, as we learned later, when the haying crews at Miller's were leaving the fields for supper, Henry, scorning both a meal and the pay due him, slipped over a fence and set out on the main road for Juniper Hill.

It was after eleven, and I was about to get ready for bed when Henry's familiar chant, clear and strong, came to me on the night breeze.

I told myself that he had "projected" himself again and that only an ectoplasmic caricature of him was chanting on the willow platform.

But I could not convince myself that such was the case. His voice was too high-pitched and powerful. There was none of the weak, tentative quality of the night before.

I set out for the knoll with many misgivings. I suppose I felt a kind of obligation to see the business through. Perhaps a sense of responsibility moved me. In addition, I will admit to a degree of curiosity.

As I started through the hemlock woods however, I experienced a feeling of acute apprehension. Henry's garbled chant, this night, was louder than I had ever heard it before. It flooded the wood. And I detected in his voice an edge of excitement bordering on hysteria.

I reached the knoll without incident and paused within the shadows cast by the surrounding hemlocks. Something seemed to warn me to keep well out of sight.

Henry, book in hand, stood on the willow platform, chanting rapidly in a shrill voice. His ring glowed more brightly than ever, bathing the book and his own face in an eerie blue light. There was a moderate wind; the tower swayed gently from side to side.

I studied the figure on the platform carefully; there was no doubt in my mind that it was Henry in the flesh. What I saw was not the projection, or apparition, of the previous night.

As he moved his head to read from the book or to look out over the black expanse of the hemlock woods, I noticed that his expression mirrored intense agitation and expectancy.

His chant rose and fell in the night, and again I sensed a frightening transformation in the contour and general appearance of the surrounding forest. Massive trees which did not resemble hemlocks seemed to loom against the darkened sky.

Once again I felt that a vast unseen audience waited among these alien trees—and that Henry was aware of their presence.

His chant swiftly became an incoherent shriek. His eyes appeared to protrude from his head; his face became so contorted it was scarcely recognizable.

I quickly became convinced that while formerly he was chanting to invoke someone or something—he was suddenly chanting frantically in an attempt to forestall the advent of whatever he had been trying to conjure.

Too late. The thing came slowly prancing and gliding over the tops of the huge fern-like trees. It was black even against the darkness of the night sky, but it seemed to contain within itself a kind of lambent flame. An aura of cold blue fire flickered about it.

If it had a definite shape, that shape was not easily apparent because it continually flowed in upon itself, contorting and writhing in a manner which I found intensely repellent.

In size, it was enormous. If you can imagine a team of six or eight black horses, somehow joined together and all attempting to gallop off in different directions at once, you might have some faint conception of the appalling thing's appearance.

Henry saw it. His shrill chanting ceased and his mouth fell open. He was frozen into immobility. His

face became wooden. Only his eyes remained
alive—two bulging points of blue light which glazed
with ultimate horror even before the monstrous entity came over the knoll.

I wanted desperately to intervene, but I was nearly
as terrified as poor Henry. And I sensed that, in any
case, I would be completely helpless if I did attempt
to interfere.

Deliberately and inexorably, the prancing nightmare made for the knoll. Once overhead, it paused.
The blue fires which animated it intesified.

It descended slowly, straight for Henry. It seemed
to tread on air, very carefully, as it came down above
him. I could detect no eyes nor mouth in the fearful
creature, but I knew that it must be equipped with a
sensory apparatus—quite probably superior to my
own.

Its convolutions almost ceased as it dropped
toward the willow platform. When it was within a
few feet of that upward-staring white face, its legs
—or whatever kind of appendages they were—
snaked down and wrapped themselves tightly about
the doomed man.

At last he was able to scream. His shriek of agony
transfixed me. It was heard all over the township of
Juniper Hill—and beyond. It would be useless for me
to attempt to convey the torment and terror which
that cry contained. I cannot.

The writhing thing ascended slowly. As it rose,
Henry almost disappeared within the hideous
seething tangle of the creature. But as it glided off,
away from the knoll, out over the tops of those enormous trees, that terrible shriek rang on and on.

The fearful intruder, flickering with fire, finally
vanished in the night, its progress marked by a tiny
trail of blue flame.

I have no clear recollection of how I groped my

way out of the woods and reached home. When Dave Baines stopped in the next morning, I was still sitting in a chair, staring at the wall. He told me later that he feared I was in shock.

At length, however, I was able to relate the events which I had witnessed just a few hours before.

Dave listened without comment, interrupting only once to tell me that Henry's final scream had awakened people all over the town.

I finished weakly, grateful for the flask of whisky which Dave had produced.

He removed his glasses and polished them carefully. "We'll never see Henry alive again—and maybe not dead either!"

I set down my glass. "But, Dave, what *was* it? I was sober and in my right mind—and yet my brain refuses to accept what it tells me I saw!"

Dave helped himself to the whisky. "Henry was tampering with malign forces, entities which probably existed when the earth was young. Nature, you know, experimented with many life forms—and not all of those forms were necessarily on the physical plane, or at least not as we know it now. Some of them probably existed and passed away, and the tenuous elements of which they were composed left no traces—certainly nothing like heavy skulls and body bones which could survive physically for millions of years.

"I think Henry summoned up, as it were, an early life form which we now vaguely refer to as an 'elemental.' In a sense, it still exists—but in another time, you might say another dimension. From what you've described, it was quite probably looked on as a god to be worshipped by earlier inhabitants of this planet. What those inhabitants were—or who they were—I can't say. Perhaps the present location of that knoll and the hemlock wood was the place of worship. And quite possibly those early worshippers offered up sacrifices to the thing which they venerated—and feared.''

Dave shook his head. ''I don't know—it's speculation. But that's all I can offer. I believe that old Hannibal Trobish was somehow involved in the business. I think both the Latin book and Henry's ring belonged to him. He may have invoked the damnable entity and survived. Probably he knew how to keep out of its clutches once it appeared. Poor Henry learned just enough Latin to chant those incantations and summon up the thing, but, obviously, he had no idea how to escape it or dismiss it once it was evoked.

''That ring *may* have been a protective talisman. But chances are the ring itself was of no help unless the intruder was placated or its powers nullified by various sacrifices and/or specific formulas. I imagine those formulas were contained somewhere in the book, but Henry hadn't really learned Latin well enough to understand how to fully protect himself against the monster he managed to call down.

''The great fern-tree forest you thought you saw—well, I don't know. It may have been a sort of telepathic image projected from the past—possibly, even, from the organ which served that creature as a brain. Even if the thing existed in another plane of the time continuum, Henry's chants undoubtedly enabled it to slip through—temporarily at least—to the present.''

Old Dave got up and moved toward the door. ''If you'd ever lived in the far north—as I did at one time—you'd know the legend of the wendigo. A lot of people today think it's sheer nonsense. But they haven't sat around a campfire at midnight and heard the best guide in Canada swear by all the saints that he had glimpsed such a thing! I don't say Henry's nightmare, necessarily, was just that—but it appears to have been a related entity.''

A week later, in a cornfield more than twenty miles from the northern edge of the township of Juniper Hill, a farmer found a bundle of bones which appeared to have passed through a blast furnace. The bones were burned to the marrow. The ghastly skeleton might have remained forever unidentifiable save for one thing—on the brittle finger bone of one hand a peculiar ring was found. In spite of the condition of the skeleton, the ring was undamaged by fire. The shining band was shaped out of a metal which resembled silver, fretted with tiny veins of blue which glowed faintly. The ring's stone was black, flat-cut, and dull in luster.

The burned remains of Henry Crotell were borne back to Juniper Hill and buried. The ring was left on the finger bone.

A few weeks later, on orders of Dave Baines, the cellar hole of the old Trobish house was filled in and leveled off.

The willow tower went down under the winds during the winter. In the spring, as improved highways were planned in Juniper Hill, a track was cut through the hemlock woods and the entire knoll which had held the willow platform was bulldozed away in order to secure its stone and gravel for the new roadbeds.

The Latin book which had led Henry to his doom was never located. I think it safe to assume that it was reduced to ashes by the same terrible fires which consumed him.

Who
Was He?

Several months ago while I was in the hospital recovering from a coronary attack, I underwent a bizarre and frightening experience which I am at a loss to explain. But I want to get the facts down before they begin to fade as most events seem to do.

After I was released from the intensive care unit, I was put in a small single room near the end of what I referred to as "coronary corridor." This corridor was long, rather narrow, and not particularly well-lighted. There were about a dozen other single rooms situated along both sides of it.

After a day or two I usually kept my door shut in order to muffle the racket of radios and television sets which came from the other rooms. I preferred to read quietly.

One day as I was reading, the door softly opened. I didn't hear it open; but I was perfectly aware, even before I looked up, that someone was standing in the doorway.

I had hoped it might be a visitor, but I saw with

disappointment and a twinge of annoyance that it was only a hospital barber. He wore a thin alpaca cloth jacket which looked a bit seedy, and he carried a small, rather disreputable black bag. Instead of speaking, he merely formed a wordless question by lifting his thick black eyebrows.

I shook my head. "Not right now. Perhaps later on."

He looked inordinately disappointed, and he lingered in the doorway a moment. Finally he turned, closing the door quietly.

For some reason I could no longer concentrate on my book. I admitted to myself, at length, that he had startled me and that this had made me angry. Not a proper state of affairs, I realized, for a coronary patient. I took a tranquilizer and tried to sleep—unsuccessfully.

I slept reasonably well that night however (with the aid of a sleeping tablet), and after various ablutions, bed-changings, temperature-takings, etc., the next morning, I settled back to my book. But I found that I was still unable to concentrate on it although it had held my attention well enough the day before. At length, as I glanced around the small room, frowning with fretfulness, I realized what the trouble was.

My door was again closed as I had requested, but now I found that I no longer wanted it closed. For the life of me, I couldn't say why. Since I was still forbidden to walk, I rang for the nurse.

A nurse's aide, a rather breezy, flaxen-haired Swedish girl, swept in. "Tired of being a hermit already? I thought you'd change your mind!" I smiled, rather sheepishly I suppose, and she went out, leaving the door open.

I returned to my book, but some buried part of my mind kept mulling over the business about the door. I finally had to admit the truth: I definitely did not want that shabby-looking hospital barber to open the door while I was reading and startle me again. The raucous screech and blare of television and radio continued to irritate me, but I tried to read over it. In this I was only partially successful.

After lunch I began to feel drowsy. I laid aside my book and was starting to doze off when a terrific, hair-raising scream lifted me upright in bed. I was sure that it had originated in one of the other nearby rooms along the corridor.

I could feel my heart pounding. I tried to tell myself that the scream had come from a television set. Someone, I assured myself, had suddenly and inadvertently turned a volume dial up to its maximum potential.

Moments later I heard a great commotion in the corridor. Nurses and orderlies rushed by. I had had no idea there were so many people on the floor. Doctors hurried past. There was a brief period of murmured commands, conversation, and then near silence. Slowly, the nurses and orderlies walked back down the corridor. A few minutes later, a still form, covered from head to foot with a rubberized sheet, was rolled past my door.

I waited a while and then rang for a nurse. The flaxen-haired Swedish nurse's aide hurried in. I had never known her to respond so swiftly before. I thought she looked a little pale.

"What happened?" I asked her.

She hesitated, then shrugged. "Mr. Caldress. Across the corridor, one room down."

"Fatal attack?"

She nodded.

I watched her face. "Isn't it—unusual—for a heart patient to cry out like that?"

Again she hesitated. When she spoke, she appeared to be choosing her words carefully. "It is—not usually the case. But, sometimes, things like that happen. Probably he, well, had a very sudden severe pain. Most patients would just—crumple over. But he managed to scream. It was—unusual.''

She smiled, rather mechanically I thought. "But don't you think about it! You are getting along fine. You read one of your good books and don't think about it.''

Of course I did think about it. I thought about it all the rest of the day and into the evening, and they finally gave me an extra sleeping tablet to settle me down.

A couple of days passed uneventfully, and then one afternoon as I was reading again with the door open I experienced the unpleasant sensation that I was being watched—closely, intensely.

I looked up. There stood the shabby hospital barber in the doorway with his sleazy alpaca jacket and his scuffed black bag. As before, the heavy black eyebrows lifted in a wordless question.

As on the previous occasion, I was angry because he had startled me. "Damn the man!" I thought. "Can't he have the common courtesy to tap on the door even though it is open?''

"I don't need a haircut!" I told him forcefully. "When I do, I'll have one of the nurses inform you!''

Still he hung in the doorway. His face looked bland, expressionless, like a mask, but the bright black eyes positively glinted with disappointment and something more than disappointment. I wasn't sure what it was. I might say resentment, but that seems too mild a word. It looked more like positive animosity.

I felt the blood rising to my neck and face. "Will you please leave?" I flung at him.

I may have imagined it, but I thought he bowed ever so slightly. A moment later he was gone.

Resolving to speak to the head nurse, I tried to settle back to my book, but it was some time before I could comprehend what I was reading.

I had begun to relax and was even looking forward to dinner when my mood was shattered by another human cry emanating from a nearby room. It was not a high-pitched scream this time. It was a moan, a subdued wail, but there was terror and hopelessness in it.

I froze, my heart thumping again. I heard a shout, then running feet. An emergency exit door at my end of the corridor opened, and I heard light but frantically running feet clattering down the fire escape. A minute later they were followed by heavy purposeful feet, pounding down three or four steps at a time.

I could not see too clearly into the corridor and, in addition, the room from which the cry had come this time was further up. But as before, I heard people rushing along, exclamations, commands, murmured conversation, and then silence.

In my mind's eye I visualized the stretcher rolling down that dim corridor once again with its silent rider beneath a gray rubberized sheet.

My Swedish nurse's aide was off that day; a new aide, a rather attractive little redhead, brought in my dinner. It was obvious that her cheerfulness was forced.

"Who was it this time?" I asked.

She was silent a moment, pretending to arrange my tray. "It was Mr. Mayerton. Room 375."

My room was 377. Mayerton's was just two rooms away.

I tried to extract more information from the new aide, but I was unsuccessful. She told me she hadn't been present, that she had heard of Mr. Mayerton's demise only a few minutes before when she first came on duty.

The next day I tried to pry more information from the other nurses. I had no luck. Either they had been instructed not to talk or they had so decided themselves. They assured me that Mayerton had died peacefully. They professed ignorance of the moan or wail which I described. They told me that Mayerton had rung for help just before lapsing into unconsciousness. If there was a cry, they insisted, it was "involuntary."

They shrugged off my question about running feet on the fire escape. I was probably drowsing, one of them said, and imagined the sounds.

I tried to forget the episode, but I was far from satisified.

That afternoon as I was reading mail, I heard a smart rap on the door. I looked up.

A neat young man with glossy hair and a toothbrush moustache stood in the doorway. He was wearing a spotless white jacket, and he carried a small beige case.

"Haircut, sir?"

I hesitated. "Well—not right now. In a day or two perhaps."

He nodded affably. "Just as you say, sir. I'll check back in a few days."

As soon as he left, I was sorry that I hadn't told him to go ahead and cut my hair. In the first place I needed a haircut. Beyond that, I wanted to question him about the other hospital barber. I hoped his shabby predecessor had left for good.

The other barber, I told myself, had "conditioned" me to give a negative response. Smiling ruefully to myself, I went back to my mail.

My recovery proceeded rapidly; before the new barber made the rounds on my floor again, I was assisted into a wheelchair one afternoon and rolled down to the solarium to sit for an hour.

While I was sitting there, looking rather bored I suppose, one of the hospital security guards strolled along. I hailed him, and he walked over for a chat.

In my somewhat unsystematic "career," I have held a number of different jobs. Some years before, for instance, I myself had worked as a part-time security guard. Very shortly, therefore, the hospital guard and I were engaged in friendly and animated conversation.

Inevitably, the conversation veered to the two recent deaths in "coronary corridor." I noticed at once that my new friend became less loquacious. He looked around uneasily a number of times to see if anyone was listening. He appeared to ponder a decision; finally he shrugged.

"If you promise not to say a single word to anybody—especially anybody here—I'll tell you a little story."

I swore on my honor not to breathe a syllable.

He frowned, not sure how to begin. "Well, there was something mighty peculiar about those deaths. First of all, both those patients were found dead with a look of fear frozen on their faces. Eyes still open and starin' as if they'd seen something so awful they'd died of fright! And both times, right after they yelled or groaned, a little guy carryin' a black bag was seen runnin' down that corridor. In fact, the second time I saw him myself. I chased him!"

I felt my heart thumping. "Can you describe him?"

"I saw him from the back mostly. Small, wiry character wearin' a thin gray jacket. Carried a crummy little black bag. I just caught a side glimpse of his face. Looked smooth, not much expression, a poker face. Thick black eyebrows."

"That's the other hospital barber!" I told him.

He stared at me. "The *other* barber? There's only one—a young guy with a toothbrush moustache. Wears a white jacket. He's been here over a year." He hesitated. "Hey, did you see this guy too?"

I waved a hand. "Never mind that now. Go on."

He scrubbed his chin. "Well, I didn't see this creep the first time, but the second time I was right there on the floor. Right after Mayerton groaned and rang for the nurse, I saw this wiry guy run out of his room. I started after him down the corridor. He bolted out the emergency door and down the fire escape.''

"Catch him?"

He shook his head. "Not a chance. He ran like a rabbit. And he went over that parking-lot fence like a deer. It took me two or three minutes to climb over; by then he was nowhere in sight.''

He looked at me. "But the craziest part is yet to come. You know that little black bag he carried?''

I nodded.

"Well, when he hopped over the fence, the bag caught on the top strand of wire and fell back in the parking lot. I picked it up later and what do you suppose I found inside?''

"I have no idea," I told him. "Don't keep me in suspense!"

"Dirt!" he answered. "Just plain dirt. Earth dirt."

As I pondered this, he went on. "And that's not all. Listen to this. When they ran in after Caldress and Mayerton died, you know what they found sprinkled on both their beds? Earth dirt!"

At this point a nurse came to return me to my room. The guard bid me a hasty goodbye, promising to look in on me later.

I didn't sleep well that night. The Swedish girl scolded me because my pressure had gone up; the night nurse said I had a temperature.

But the final denouement was yet to come. I was sitting in the solarium a few days later, feeling quite chipper (the young barber had just given me an expert haircut) when the security guard came along.

He sat down, looking around warily. "I probably shouldn't tell you this, but I might as well finish the story.''

"Please do!" I urged him.

"Well, I had to turn in that little black bag full of earth, but before the police got it, I filled a paper sack with some of the dirt. I gave it to a friend of mine who works in a laboratory. He's got a microscope and all kinds of testing stuff. You know what he found out?"

"I can't imagine!"

He leaned closer. "That dirt, that earth dirt—he swears it must have come out of a cemetery."

I felt my heart thumping again, but I pretended that I was skeptical. "Oh, how could he tell that?"

"From little bits of things that he found mixed in the dirt. Tiny chips of marble and granite like from gravestones. Bits of artificial flowers and wreaths. And not only that. He says there were even a couple of little bone splinters that check out as human! And all the dirt was mixed with moss and mold as if it had been dug out of a wet, dark corner of the cemetery."

That's the story and I can offer no explanation. The wiry little man with the mask-like face, the glittering eyes, and the heavy black eyebrows was never seen again.

A certain friend of mine, who considers himself quite a clever fellow, says the explanation is obvious. The man with the black bag, he tells me, was a typical psychopath who was either born with a terribly disfigured face or acquired one in some horrible accident. Wearing a mask, he slipped into the coronary unit and literally frightened the two patients to death by merely entering their rooms and whipping off his mask. My friend says that the sprinkling of cemetery earth on the beds was only a macabre whim generated by a twisted mind.

This explanation may sound plausible, but I myself feel certain that for some obscure psychic reason, the frightful creature whom I mistook for the hospital barber was powerless to enter a patient's room unless bidden to do so. I believe that both heart patients who cried out and died gave him permission to come into their rooms. No one, of course, seemed to remember whether or not they needed haircuts! I cannot explain my conviction. It remains with me; that is all.

I will add only this. I am quite positive in my own mind that if I had given that lethal intruder assent to enter my room, you would not be reading this story—because I am sure that I would not have lived to write it.

Disappearance

At the time of Dan Mellmer's disappearance I happened to be a deputy, and Sheriff Kellington asked me to accompany him when he drove over to the Mellmer place to investigate.

We both thought at the time that we might be faced with murder. The two Mellmer brothers, Dan and Russell, had quarreled bitterly for years. It was no secret that they hated each other. They remained on their big farm together because they had inherited it jointly and because each was too stubborn to sell out to the other and depart. Dan had often threatened to leave—after he had burned down every building on the farm—but nobody ever believed that he finally would.

But perhaps he had actually left without fulfilling his promise to burn out his brother. Either that or Russell had killed him.

On the way over, Sheriff Kellington admitted he had often felt that the situation at the Mellmer place was a potentially explosive one. The two brothers were middle-aged, ingrown, and eccentric. Each blamed the other for his indifferent status in life and neither would cooperate for the common benefit of both. Living under the same roof month after month and year after year, continually grating on each other's nerves, anything could happen.

Russell Mellmer had telephoned the Sheriff that morning and reported Dan's disappearance. He had sounded casual and unconcerned, the Sheriff said, and had emphasized that he was not reporting the disappearance because of worry or brotherly solicitude but solely to keep himself clear of suspicion.

It was late December and piercingly cold. Although only scattered scarves of snow lay on the ground, the earth was frozen like granite. The ruts on the dirt road leading to the Mellmer place were as unyielding as iron.

Driving along past desolate fields where not even a crow was visible, we soon came in sight of the Mellmer farmhouse. When we turned into the driveway, the prevailing bleakness of our surroundings remained. The unpainted house with its loose, rattling clapboards and the unkempt front yard, overgrown with beards of brown grass, heightened the atmosphere of general desolation.

Russell Mellmer met us at the door. He was a tall man, bony and angular, with a turn to his long jaw which gave him a sardonic, quizzical expression. If he had changed his overalls and corduroy jacket for trousers and an alpaca coat, he might have passed for a country school teacher or the village postmaster.

When we were seated inside, he told his story. It was very simple. His brother Dan had gone to his room at ten o'clock the night before. That morning he was missing. He had left no note, and he had taken only the clothes which he customarily wore.

When Russell Mellmer finished his brief and

unembroidered account, he got up, opened the big pot-belly stove, already glowing red, and dropped another chunk of coal inside.

Sheriff Kellington frowned. "But why would he leave in weather like this—in the middle of the night—and where would he go?"

Mellmer shrugged. "Who knows? I've often thought lately that he was getting weak in the head. And he's threatened to leave often enough. Everybody knows that. I guess he just suddenly made up his mind and lit out."

Sheriff Kellington wasn't satisfied and neither was I. With Mellmer's ready permission, we made a thorough search of the house and the nearby barns and sheds, but we found nothing amiss.

The Sheriff kicked absently at a wagon wheel as we came out of the barn. "Maybe Dan really did take off, but I'll feel better when we have some proof of it."

We stood looking out over the fields behind the Mellmer farmhouse. The back of the house faced a stony pasture and beyond that lay the frosted and tattered remnants of a summer's cornfield. A forlorn scarecrow flapped in the wind at the far end of the field.

We entered the pasture and poked among the weathered gray boulders. A little brook which ran through the lot was frozen solid. We went on into the cornfield and walked around, listening to the wind whisper and moan among the dry stalks.

Sheriff Kellington tested the heel of his heavy boot against the hard earth. "Anyway, nobody could be buried in this ground. You'd need a load of dynamite to dig a grave."

It was true. The earth was like stone. It would take a man days to dig a grave. Even with dynamite it would be no easy task. And at no point could we find that the earth had been so much as scratched.

We gave up finally and went back to town where the Sheriff made out his official report and began further inquiries.

Several days passed, but no word of Dan Mellmer came in. No one had seen him leave the town area, and there was no report to indicate that he had been spotted elsewhere. Russell Mellmer stuck to his original story and had nothing further to add.

Sheriff Kellington confided his uneasiness to me. Both the Mellmers were fairly well-known in the county, and it seemed unlikely that Dan could have gotten completely away without having been observed by someone.

At length Sheriff Kellington, four temporary deputies, and I descended on the Mellmer farm for another search.

This time we really ransacked the place. Every building was scoured from roof to cellar. We even removed some of the hay that was stacked in the barn. Sheriff Kellington had one of the deputies walk up and down every single row of the cornfield. The deputy carried out his task in the freezing wind and found nothing.

Neither did anyone else. And all the time Russell Mellmer stood by, silent, sardonic, and unruffled.

We returned to town that evening, aching and half-numbed with cold. While we had whiskey in the Sheriff's office, he admitted that so far as he was concerned the search was at an end. Unless new developments transpired, he felt justified in assuming that Dan Mellmer had voluntarily left for parts unknown.

But I felt that he was still not satisfied. He had the frustrated air of a man trying to dismiss from his mind a riddle he is unable to solve.

For a number of months Dan Mellmer's disappearance was the chief topic of conversation among the town gossips. Conjectures and speculations were bandied back and forth at a lively rate. Opinions seemed to be about evenly divided. Some thought that Russell had very definitely had a hand in his brother's disappearance. Others, recalling Dan's frequent threats to "light out," scoffed at the idea.

Gradually the matter was forgotten. The town gossips found other topics of interest. Jed Heller's house burned down; Frank Massing had most of his head blown off in a hunting accident; Miss Brett, the forty-year-old "school mar'm" eloped with a sailor half her age. And so it went.

I had been on friendly enough terms with both Mellmer brothers before Dan's disappearance, and while I seldom visited them because of the explosive atmosphere generated by their mutual antagonism, I did usually manage to stop in for a brief chat once or twice a year. So, one October day a good ten months after Dan had vanished, I decided to stop around and pay Russell Mellmer a visit.

I had no idea how he would receive me because he rarely came into town and I hadn't seen him except at a distance since the time Sheriff Kellington and we deputies searched the place. But I didn't want him to think that I harbored any ill will toward him. There was not, after all, one shred of concrete proof that he had physically molested his brother Dan. And I wanted him to know that so far as I was concerned he was presumed innocent.

Autumn was nearing the climax of its annual color carnival when I drove around to pay my visit that afternoon. Even the Mellmer premises, in a somewhat ragged way, looked attractive. Wild blue gentians were growing in the dooryard and a swirl of enameled oak leaves had settled by the door.

Russell Mellmer was obviously surprised when he answered my knock. His eyes narrowed a little and that familiar sardonic smile touched his face. "Business?" he inquired.

I shook my head. "Just passing by," I lied mildly. "Thought I'd stop a minute. If you're busy—"

He opened the door wider. "No. No. Come on in. Nice weather we're having."

I stepped in and sat down, and we went on talking about the weather and the past summer's crops and what kind of a winter we might expect. He was polite and appeared friendly enough, and yet I sensed an element of constraint in the room. Whether it was my own or his I couldn't quite decide.

He looked older and leaner than he had the last time I saw him. I thought at times that an obscure expression of caution, of shiftiness almost, crept into his face. Yet that quizzical grin of his came often enough, and not infrequently he chuckled with genuine amusement.

When I had been there about ten minutes he suggested a drink of whiskey, and although I didn't particularly want one, I agreed out of politeness.

He seemed to enjoy his drink and had another which I refused.

In spite of the whisky, however, our conversation rather quickly dwindled away, and I began to feel uncomfortable. After coming in from the crisp autumn air outside, the atmosphere of the room itself seemed to become gradually oppressive.

From where I sat I could look beyond the boulder-strewn pasture behind the house and out across the cornfield. A flock of glossy black crows flew diagonally over the field, broke ranks, and settled among the rows. One of them perched jauntily on an outstretched arm of the ragged scarecrow at the far end of the lot.

It was a typical autumn scene, all russet and bronze with a blurred misty blueness about the edges of things, and yet for some reason which I couldn't name I was suddenly seized with a feeling of utter desolation. It wasn't the mellow, reminiscent nostalgia which ought to go with October. It was dismal, bleak.

I stood up rather suddenly I'm afraid, and for just a moment I thought that I detected a look of alarm on my host's face.

But perhaps I only imagined it. He bid me good day pleasantly enough, and if it appeared to me that he seemed relieved at my departure, possibly it was only my own relief which was reflected back to me.

I never visited Russell Mellmer again. As one year grew into two, and two lengthened to five, I must admit that I experienced a twinge of self-reproach. But the unpleasant memory of my last visit remained vivid in my mind. And, in any case, I felt that Russell Mellmer didn't particularly care whether I stopped by or not.

As the years hurried past, he became increasingly eccentric. Never gregarious, he finally came to live almost like a hermit, walking into town only on rare occasions. He became more taciturn than ever. Although he usually declined to converse, he had no objection to the role of passive listener. During his infrequent trips to town, he sometimes sat for a while in the general store and listened to the other loafers talk. Once in a while something in the conversation would bring that odd sardonic grin back to his face.

Once Sheriff Kellington had a brief encounter with him after he had fired a load of buckshot at some boys whom he asserted had been stealing pumpkins from his cornfield. The Sheriff warned him not to repeat the performance, but the boys never went back and that ended the matter.

Nothing was ever heard of Dan Mellmer. Russell never mentioned him, and as time went on, scarcely anyone else did either.

Ten years and some eight months after Dan's disappearance, Russell Mellmer telephoned into town for a doctor, but he was dead of a heart attack before Doc Luder arrived.

The final ceremonies were simple and brief. Most of the town turned out for the funeral, and of course the subject of Dan's disappearance was revived. Someone suggested that Russell might have left some message which would explain his brother's strange drop from sight nearly eleven years before.

But no written message of any kind was found. In fact, Russell Mellmer had not even bothered to draw up a will. The farm went into probate, and there was some attempt to locate the usual "distant relatives" who nobody was sure really existed.

One afternoon in early November, nearly two months after the funeral, Sheriff Kellington drove up to my place and rang the bell.

I was mildly surprised to see him. Because of the press of other work, I had relinquished the deputy sheriff job a few years before. Although the Sheriff and I remained on the best of terms, he seldom called on me.

He greeted me pleasantly, but he appeared uneasy and even embarrassed. For a moment he just stood there, turning his hat around in his hands."

"I just wondered," he said, "if you're too busy to take a little ride with me—unofficial like?"

Although I had no idea what he had in mind, I readily agreed. Ten minutes later we were riding out of town.

Most of the leaves had already fallen, and the land was quickly acquiring the barren look of winter. A cold wind blew out of a slate-colored sky.

Sheriff Kellington frowned at the passing fields. "This may be just a fool's errand," he said. "In a way, I hope it is."

"What's the destination?" I asked.

"The Mellmer place." He glanced at me

enigmatically. "You were with me on the case when Dan disappeared over ten years ago—and that's why I wanted you to come along today."

"Russell Mellmer left some evidence then?"

He shrugged. "Don't know yet. Here's what happened. Since Russell died, some of the kids from town have been poking around the place. You know how he used to drive them away. Now that he's gone, they've taken to romping all over the property. Well—this morning a couple of them got scared . . . ."

He let the sentence run on unfinished and I looked at him. "Sounds like a ghost!"

He didn't even grin at that. "Or something worse," he said.

He added no more, and in a few minutes we drove up in front of the Mellmer place. In the gloomy November afternoon it looked like a haunted house. Several of the windows were broken and, judging by the sound, every other clapboard on the structure was rattling in the wind.

We got out of the car, and Sheriff Kellington started around the side of the house. "What scared those kids," he said, "was in the old cornfield."

I followed him through the stony little pasture in back of the house and on into the neglected remains of the cornfield. Stubs and stalks of corn plants lay scattered about along with a wild array of weeds, vines, and withered grass.

The Sheriff pushed straight on through the tangle with scarcely a glance at the ground. Completely mystified by now, I hurried along behind him. By the time he neared the end of the field, I was beginning to lose my breath.

He stopped suddenly, and I saw that he was staring intently at the ragged shape of a scarecrow which stood a few yards away.

I glanced at the scarecrow and then at him.

"That's what frightened the kids?"

He nodded. "Let's take a look."

We walked up to the scarecrow. It appeared harmless enough—just a lot of old clothes draped around a frame of some kind with a big slouch hat jammed far down over whatever served as a head. The hat was tipped at an odd angle, as if it might have been recently disturbed.

Sheriff Kellington reached up and, after some tugging, lifted it off.

Underneath was no broom but an unmistakable human skull, weathered, gray, and grinning.

"Dan Mellmer," the Sheriff said.

I don't know how long we stood there staring at it. I guess we were both remembering back to that December day over ten years before when we had looked around in the cornfield for some sign of Dan. There had been a scarecrow in the same place then.

The Sheriff broke the silence first. "It was here all the time. It was here when we first came into the field. It was here that day I had the deputy walk up and down every row. And it's been here for ten years since."

I remembered my visit with Russell Mellmer the year after Dan vanished, and I shuddered.

A closer inspection of the ghastly thing disclosed an entire mummified skeleton, swathed and hidden under layers of ragged clothes. It was securely wired, crucifixion style, to a stout wooden frame. Some of the bones had been wired to each other also, and such care had been taken that hardly a finger joint had fallen off. It was pretty obvious that the wiring had been carefully renewed and reinforced year after year.

When the whole hideous thing was exposed to view, we stepped back and surveyed it again. I think both of us were a little sick with horror.

"I suppose," the Sheriff said, "you might almost

call it the perfect crime—so obvious we couldn't see it.''

I wanted to look away, but the thing held my gaze. "But why didn't he bury it when the searching was over?"

The Sheriff shrugged. "Maybe he liked to stand at his sitting-room window and look at it."

"Maybe," I suggested, "Dan died a natural death and—"

The Sheriff shook his head. "Look here." Striding up, he pointed to the back of the skull.

A segment of the bone a good three inches in diameter had been shattered with such force there was a ragged hole in the skull.

"Offhand I'd say an axe," Sheriff Kellington said. "Or maybe a sledge hammer. I guess we'll never know for sure."

We came away then, out of that desolate field where the cold November winds whispered among the broken corn stalks and the brown, withered weeds.

The
Horror
at
Chilton Castle

I had decided to spend a leisurely summer in Europe, concentrating, if at all, on genealogical research. I went first to Ireland, journeying to Kilkenny where I unearthed a mine of legend and authentic lore concerning my remote Irish ancestors, the O'Branonains, chiefs of Ui Duach in the ancient kingdom of Ossory. The Brennans (as the name was later spelled) lost their estates in the British confiscation under Thomas Wentworth, Earl of Strafford. The thieving Earl, I am happy to report, was subsequently beheaded in the Tower.

From Kilkenny I traveled to London and then to Chesterfield in search of maternal ancestors, the Holborns, Wilkersons, Searles, etc. Incomplete and fragmentary records left many great gaps, but my efforts were moderately successful and at length I decided to go further north and visit the vicinity of Chilton Castle, seat of Robert Chilton-Payne, the twelfth Earl of Chilton. My relationship to the Chilton-Paynes was a most distant one, and yet there existed a tenuous thread of past connection and I thought it would amuse me to glimpse the castle.

Arriving in Wexwold, the tiny village near the castle, late in the afternoon, I engaged a room at the Inn of the Red Goose—the only one there was—unpacked and went down for a simple meal consisting of a small loaf, cheese, and ale.

By the time I finished this stark and yet satisfying repast, darkness had set in, and with it came wind and rain.

I resigned myself to an evening at the inn. There was ale enough, and I was in no hurry to go anywhere.

After writing a few letters, I went down and ordered a pint of ale. The taproom was almost deserted; the bartender, a stout gentleman who seemed forever on the point of falling asleep, was pleasant but taciturn. At length I fell to musing on the strange and frightening legend of Chilton Castle.

There were variations of the legend. Without doubt the original tale had been embroidered down through the centuries, but the essential outline of the story concerned a secret room somewhere in the castle. It was said that this room contained a terrifying spectacle which the Chilton-Paynes were obliged to keep hidden from the world.

Only three persons were ever permitted to enter the room: the presiding Earl of Chilton, the Earl's male heir, and one other person designated by the Earl. Ordinarily this person was the Factor of Chilton Castle. The room was entered only once in a generation; within three days after the male heir came of age, he was conducted to the secret room by the Earl and the Factor. The room was then sealed and never opened again until the heir conducted his own son to the grisly chamber.

According to the legend, the heir was never the same person again after entering the room. Invariably he would become somber and withdrawn; his countenance would acquire a brooding, apprehensive expression which nothing could long dispell. One of the earlier earls of Chilton had gone completely mad and hurled himself from the turrets of the castle.

Speculation about the contents of the secret room had continued for centuries. One version of the tale described the panic-stricken flight of the Gowers with armed enemies hot on their flagging heels. Although there had been bad blood between the Chilton-Paynes and the Gowers, in their desperation the Gowers begged for refuge at Chilton Castle. The Earl gave them entry, conducted them to a hidden room and left with a promise that they would be shielded from their pursuers. The Earl kept his promise; the Gowers' enemies were turned away from the Castle, their murderous plans unconsummated. The Earl, however, simply left the Gowers in the locked room to starve to death. The chamber was not opened until thirty years later when the Earl's son finally broke the seal. A fearful sight met his eyes. The Gowers had starved to death slowly, and at the last, judging by the appearance of the mingled skeletons, had turned to cannibalism.

Another version of the legend indicated that the secret room had been used by medieval earls as a torture chamber. It was said that the ingenious instruments of pain were yet in the room and that these lethal apparatuses still clutched the pitiful remains of their final victims, twisted fearfully in their last agonies.

A third version mentioned one of the female ancestors of the Chilton-Paynes, Lady Susan Glanville who had reputedly made a pact with the Devil. She had been condemned as a witch but had somehow managed to escape the stake. The date and even the manner of her death were unknown, but in some vague way the secret room was supposed to be connected with it.

As I speculated on these different versions of the gruesome legend, the storm increased in intensity. Rain drummed steadily against the leaded windows of the inn, and now I could occasionally hear the distant mutter of thunder.

Glancing at the rain-streaked panes, I shrugged and ordered another pint of ale.

I had the fresh tankard halfway to my lips when the taproom door burst open, letting in a blast of wind and rain. The door was shut, and a tall figure muffled to the ears in a dripping greatcoat moved to the bar. Removing his cap, he ordered brandy.

Having nothing better to do, I observed him closely. He looked about seventy, grizzled and weather-worn, but wiry, with an appearance of toughness and determination. He was frowning as if absorbed in thinking through some unpleasant problem, yet his cold blue eyes inspected me keenly for a brief but deliberate interval.

I could not place him in a tidy niche. He might be a local farmer, and yet I did not think that he was. He had a vague aura of authority. Though his clothes were certainly plain, they were, I thought, somewhat better in cut and quality than those of the area countrymen whom I had observed.

A trivial incident opened a conversation between us. An unusually sharp crack of thunder made him turn toward the window. As he did so, he accidentally brushed his wet cap onto the floor. I retrieved it for him; he thanked me; and then we exchanged commonplace remarks about the weather.

I had an intuitive feeling that although he was a normally reticent individual, he was presently wrestling with some severe problem which made him want to hear a human voice. Realizing there was always the possibility that my intuition might have for once failed me, I nevertheless babbled on about my trip, about my genealogical researches in Kilkenny, London, and Chesterfield, and finally about my distant relationship to the Chilton-Paynes and my desire to get a good look at Chilton Castle.

Suddenly I found that he was gazing at me with an expression which, if not fierce, was disturbingly intense. An awkward silence ensued. I coughed, wondering uneasily what I had said to make those cold blue eyes stare at me so fixedly.

At length he became aware of my growing embarrassment. "You must excuse me for staring," he apologized, "but something you said. . . ." He hesitated. "Could we perhaps take that table?" He nodded toward a small table which sat half in shadow in the far corner of the room.

I agreed, mystified but curious, and we took our drinks to the secluded table.

He sat frowning for a minute as if uncertain how to begin. Finally he introduced himself as William Cowath. I gave him my name, and still he hesitated. At length he took a swallow of brandy and then looked straight at me. "I am," he stated, "the Factor at Chilton Castle."

I surveyed him with surprise and renewed interest. "What an agreeable coincidence!" I exclaimed. "Then perhaps tomorrow you could arrange for me to have a look at the castle?"

He seemed scarcely to hear me. "Yes, yes, of course," he replied absently.

Puzzled and a bit irritated by his air of detachment, I remained silent.

He took a deep breath and then spoke rapidly, running some of his words together. "Robert Chilton-Payne, the Twelfth Earl of Chilton, was buried in the family vaults one week ago. Frederick, the young heir and now Thirteenth Earl, came of age just three days ago. Tonight it is imperative that he be conducted to the secret chamber!''

I gaped at him in incredulous amazement. For a moment I had an idea that he had somehow heard of my interest in Chilton Castle and was merely "pulling my leg" for amusement in the belief that I was the greenest of gullible tourists.

But there could be no mistaking his deadly seriousness. There was not the faintest suspicion of humor in his eyes.

I groped for words. "It seems so strange—so unbelievable! Just before you arrived, I had been thinking about the various legends connected with the secret room."

His cold eyes held my own. "It is not legend that confronts us; it is fact."

A thrill of fear and excitement ran through me. "You are going there—tonight?"

He nodded. "Tonight. Myself, the young Earl—and one other."

I stared at him.

"Ordinarily," he continued, "the Earl himself would accompany us. That is the custom. But he is dead. Shortly before he passed away, he instructed me to select someone to go with the young Earl and myself. That person must be male—and preferably of the blood."

I took a deep drink of ale and said not a word.

He continued. "Besides the young Earl, there is no one at the Castle save his elderly mother, Lady Beatrice Chilton, and an ailing aunt."

"Who could the Earl have had in mind?" I inquired cautiously.

The Factor frowned. "There are some distant male cousins residing in the country. I have an idea he thought at least one of them might appear for the obsequies. But not one of them did."

"That was most unfortunate!" I observed.

"Extremely unfortunate. And I am therefore asking you, as one of the blood, to accompany the young Earl and myself to the secret room tonight!"

I gulped like a bumpkin. Lightning flashed against the windows, and I could hear rain swishing along the stones outside. When feathers of ice stopped fluttering in my stomach, I managed a reply.

"But I—that is—my relationship is so very remote! I am 'of the blood' only by courtesy, you might say! The strain in me is so very diluted!"

He shrugged. "You bear the name. And you possess at least a few drops of the Payne blood. Under the present urgent circumstances, no more is necessary. I am sure that Earl Robert would agree with me, could he still speak. You will come?"

There was no escaping the intensity, the pressure, of those cold blue eyes. They seemed to follow my mind about as it groped for further excuses.

Finally, inevitably it seemed, I agreed. A feeling grew in me that the meeting had been preordained, that, somehow, I had always been destined to visit the secret chamber in Chilton Castle.

We finished our drinks, and I went up to my room for rainwear. When I descended, suitably attired, the obese bartender was snoring on his stool in spite of savage crashes of thunder which had now become almost incessant. I envied him as I left the cozy room with William Cowath.

Once outside, my guide informed me that we would have to go afoot to the castle. He had purposely walked down to the inn, he explained, in order that he might have time and solitude to straighten out in his own mind the things which he would have to do.

The sheets of heavy rain, the strong wind, and the roar of thunder made conversation difficult. I walked Indian-fashion behind the Factor who took enormous strides and appeared to know every inch of the way in spite of the darkness.

We walked only a short distance down the village street and then struck into a side road which very soon dwindled to a footpath made slippery and treacherous by the driving rain.

Abruptly the path began to ascend; the footing became more precarious. It was at once necessary to concentrate all one's attention on one's feet. Fortunately, the flashes of lightning were frequent.

It seemed to me that we had been walking for an hour—actually, I suppose, it was only a few minutes—when the Factor finally stopped.

I found myself standing beside him on a flat rocky plateau. He pointed up an incline which rose before us. "Chilton Castle," he said.

For a moment I saw nothing in the unrelieved darkness. Then the lightning flashed.

Beyond high battlemented walls, fissured with age, I glimpsed a great square Norman castle. Four rectangular corner towers were pierced by narrow window apertures which looked like evil slitted eyes. The huge weathered pile was half covered by a mantle of ivy more black than green.

"It looks incredibly old!" I commented.

William Cowath nodded. "It was begun in 1122 by Henry de Montargis." Without another word he started up the incline.

As we approached the castle wall, the storm grew worse. The slanting rain and powerful wind now made speech impossible. We bent our heads and staggered upward.

When the wall finally loomed in front of us, I was amazed at its height and thickness. It had been constructed, obviously, to withstand the best siege guns and battering rams which its early enemies could bring to bear on it.

As we crossed a massive timbered drawbridge, I

peered down into the black ditch of a moat, but I could not be sure whether there was water in it. A low arched gateway gave access through the wall to an inner cobblestoned courtyard. This courtyard was entirely empty save for rivulets of rushing water.

Crossing the cobblestones with swift strides, the Factor led me to another arched gateway in yet another wall. Inside was a second smaller yard and beyond spread the ivy-clutched base of the ancient keep itself.

Traversing a darkened stone-flagged passage, we found ourselves facing a ponderous door, age-blackened oak reinforced with pitted bands of iron. The Factor flung open this door, and there before us was the great hall of the castle.

Four long hand-hewn tables with their accompanying benches stretched almost the entire length of the hall. Metal torch brackets, stained with age, were affixed to sculptured stone columns which supported the roof. Ranged around the walls were suits of armor, heraldic shields, halberds, pikes, and banners—the accumulated trophies and prizes of bloody centuries when each castle was almost a kingdom unto itself. In flickering candlelight, which appeared to be the only illumination, the grim array was eerily impressive.

William Cowath waved a hand. "The holders of Chilton lived by the sword for many centuries."

Walking the length of the great hall, he entered another dim passageway. I followed silently.

As we strode along, he spoke in a subdued voice. "Frederick, the young heir, does not enjoy robust health. The shock of his father's death was severe —and he dreads tonight's ordeal which he knows must come."

Stopping before a wooden door embellished with carved fleurs-de-lis and metal scrollwork, he gave me a shadowed, enigmatic glance and then knocked.

Someone inquired who was there and he identified himself. Presently a heavy bolt was lifted. The door opened.

If the Chilton-Paynes had been stubborn fighters in their day, the warrior blood appeared to have become considerably diluted in the veins of Frederick, the young heir and now Thirteenth Earl. I saw before me a thin, pale young man whose dark, sunken eyes looked haunted and fearful. His dress was both theatrical and anachronistic: a dark green velvet coat and trousers, a green satin waistband, flounces of white lace at neck and wrists.

He beckoned us in, as if with reluctance, and closed the door. The walls of the small room were entirely covered with tapestries depicting the hunt or medieval battle scenes. Drafts of air from a window or other aperture made them undulate constantly; they seemed to have a disturbing life of their own. In one corner of the room there was an antique canopy bed; in another a large writing table with an agate lamp.

After a brief introduction, which included an explanation of how I came to be accompanying them, the Factor inquired if his Lordship was ready to visit the chamber.

Although he was wan in any case, Earl Frederick's face now lost every last trace of color. He nodded, however, and preceded us into the passage.

William Cowath led the way; the Earl followed him; and I brought up the rear.

At the far end of the passage, the Factor opened the door of a cobwebbed supply room. Here he secured candles, chisels, a pick, and a sledgehammer. After packing these into a leather bag which he slung over one shoulder, he picked up a faggot torch which lay on one of the shelves in the room. He lit this, waiting while it flared into a steady flame. Satisfied with this illumination, he closed the room and beckoned for us to continue after him.

Nearby was a descending spiral of stone steps. Lifting his torch, the Factor started down. We trailed after him wordlessly.

There must have been fifty steps in that long downward spiral. As we descended, the stones became wet and cold; the air, too, grew colder. It was laden with the smell of mold and dampness.

At the bottom of the steps we faced a tunnel, pitch-black and silent.

The Factor raised his torch. "Chilton Castle is Norman but is said to have been reared over a Saxon ruin. It is believed that the passageways in these depths were constructed by the Saxons.". He peered, frowning, into the tunnel. "Or by some still earlier folk."

He hesitated briefly, and I thought he was listening. Then, glancing round at us, he proceeded down the passage.

I walked after the Earl, shivering. The dead, icy air seemed to pierce to the pith of my bones. The stones underfoot grew slick with a film of slime. I longed for more light, but there was none save that cast by the flickering, bobbing torch of the Factor.

Partway down the passage he paused, and again I sensed that he was listening. The silence seemed absolute, however, and we went on.

The end of the passage brought us to more descending steps. We went down some fifteen and entered another tunnel which appeared to have been cut out of the solid rock on which the castle had been built. White-crusted nitre clung to the walls. The reek of mold was intense. The icy air was fetid with some other odor which I found peculiarly repellent, though I could not name it.

At last the Factor stopped, lifted his torch and slid the leather bag from his shoulder.

I saw that we stood before a wall made of some

kind of building stone. Though damp and stained with nitre, it was obviously of much more recent construction than anything we had previously encountered.

Glancing round at us, William Cowath handed me the torch. "Keep a good hold on it, if you please. I have candles, but—"

Leaving the sentence unfinished, he drew the pick from his sling bag and began an assault on the wall. The barrier was solid enough, but after he had worked a hole in it, he took up the sledgehammer and quicker progress was made. Once I offered to take up the sledge while he held the torch, but he only shook his head and went on with his work of demolition.

All this time the young Earl had not spoken a word. As I looked at his tense white face, I felt sorry for him in spite of my own mounting trepidation.

Abruptly there was silence as the Factor lowered the sledgehammer. I saw that a good two feet of the lower wall remained.

William Cowath bent to inspect it. "Strong enough," he commented cryptically. "I will leave that to build on. We can step over it."

For a full minute he stood looking silently into the blackness beyond. Finally, shouldering his bag, he took the torch from my hand and stepped over the ragged base of the wall. We followed suit.

As I entered that chamber, the fetid odor which I had noticed in the passage seemed to overwhelm us. It washed around us in a nauseating wave, and we all gasped for breath.

The Factor spoke between coughs. "It will subside in a minute or two. Stand near the aperture."

Although the reek remained repellently strong, we could at length breathe more freely.

William Cowath lifted his torch and peered into the black depths of the chamber. Fearfully, I gazed around his shoulder.

There was no sound and at first I could see nothing but nitre-encrusted walls and wet stone floor. Presently, however, in a far corner, just beyond the flickering halo of the faggot torch, I saw two tiny fiery spots of red. I tried to convince myself that they were two red jewels, two rubies, shining in the torchlight.

But I knew at once—I *felt* at once—what they were. They were two red eyes, and they were watching us with a fierce unwavering stare.

The Factor spoke softly. "Wait here."

He crossed toward the corner, stopped halfway and held out his torch at arm's length. For a moment he was silent. Finally he emitted a long shuddering sigh.

When he spoke again, his voice had changed. It was only a sepulchral whisper. "Come forward," he told us in that strange hollow voice.

I followed Earl Frederick until we stood at either side of the Factor.

When I saw what crouched on a stone bench in that far corner, I felt sure that I would faint. My heart literally stopped beating for perceptible seconds. The blood left my extremities; I reeled with dizziness. I might have cried out, but my throat would not open.

The entity which rested on that stone bench was like something that had crawled up out of hell. Piercing malignant red eyes proclaimed that it had a terrible life, and yet that life sustained itself in a black, shrunken half-mummified body which resembled a disinterred corpse. A few moldy rags clung to the cadaver-like frame. Whisps of white hair sprouted out of its ghastly gray-white skull. A red smear or blotch of some sort covered the wizened slit which served it as a mouth.

It surveyed us with a malignancy which was beyond anything merely human. It was impossible to stare back into those monstrous red eyes. They were so inexpressibly evil, one felt that one's soul would be consumed in the fires of their malevolence.

Glancing aside, I saw that the Factor was now supporting Earl Frederick. The young heir had sagged against him. The Earl stared fixedly at the fearful apparition with terror-glazed eyes. In spite of my own sense of horror, I pitied him.

The Factor sighed again, and then he spoke once more in that low sepuchral voice.

"You see before you," he told us, "Lady Susan Glanville. She was carried into this chamber and fettered to the wall in 1473."

A thrill of horror coursed through me; I felt that we were in the presence of malign forces from the Pit itself.

To me the hideous thing had appeared sexless, but at the sound of its name, the ghastly mockery of a grin contorted the puckered red-smeared mouth.

I noticed now for the first time that the monster actually was secured to the wall. The great double shackles were so blackened with age that I had not noticed them before.

The Factor went on, speaking as if by rote. "Lady Glanville was a maternal ancestor of the Chilton-Paynes. She had commerce with the Devil. She was condemned as a witch but escaped the stake. Finally her own people forcibly overcame her. She was brought in here, fettered, and left to die."

He was silent a moment and then continued. "It was too late. She had already made a pact with the Powers of Darkness. It was an unspeakably evil thing, and it has condemned her issue to a life of torment and nightmare, a lifetime of terror and dread."

He swung his torch toward the blackened red-eyed thing. "She was a beauty once. She hated death. She feared death. And so she finally bartered her own immortal soul—and the bodies of her issue—for eternal earthly life.''

I heard his voice as in a nightmare; it seemed to be coming from an infinite distance.

He went on. "The consequences of breaking the pact are too terrible to describe. No descendant of hers has ever dared to do so, once the forfeit is known. And so she had bided here for these nearly five hundred years.''

I had thought he was finished, but he resumed. Glancing upward, he lifted his torch toward the roof of that accursed chamber. "This room,'' he said, "lies directly underneath the family vaults. Upon the death of the male Earl, the body is ostensibly left in the vaults. When the mourners have gone, however, the false bottom of the vault is thrust aside and the body of the Earl is lowered into this room.''

Looking up, I saw the square rectangle of a trap door above.

The Factor's voice now became barely audible. "Once every generation Lady Glanville feeds—on the corpse of the deceased Earl. It is a provision of that unspeakable pact which cannot be broken.''

I knew now—with a sense of horror utterly beyond description—whence came that red smear on the repulsive mouth of the creature before us.

As if to confirm his words, the Factor lowered his torch until its flame illuminated the floor at the foot of the stone bench where the vampiric monster was fettered.

Strewn about the floor were the scattered bones and skull of an adult male, red with fresh blood. And at some distance were other human bones, brown and crumbling with age.

At this point young Earl Frederick began to scream. His shrill hysterical cries filled the chamber. Although the Factor shook him roughly, his terrible shrieks continued, terror-filled, nerve-shaking.

For moments the corpse-like thing on the bench watched him with its frightful red eyes. It uttered sound finally, a kind of animal squeal which might have been intended as laughter.

Abruptly then, and without any warning, it slid from the bench and lunged toward the young Earl. The blackened shackles which fettered it to the wall permitted it to advance only a yard or two. It was pulled back sharply; yet it lunged again and again, squealing with a kind of hellish glee which stirred the hair on my head.

William Cowath thrust his torch toward the monster, but it continued to lunge at the end of its fetters. The nightmare room resounded with the Earl's screams and the creature's horrible squeals of bestial laughter. I felt that my own mind would give way unless I escaped from that anteroom of hell.

For the first time during an ordeal which would have sent any lesser man fleeing for his life and sanity, the iron control of the Factor appeared to be shaken. He looked beyond the wild lunging thing toward the wall where the fetters were fastened.

I sensed what was in his mind. Would those fastenings hold, after all these centuries of rust and dampness?

On a sudden resolve he reached into an inner pocket and drew out something which glittered in the torchlight. It was a silver crucifix. Striding forward, he thrust it almost into the twisted face of the leaping monstrosity which had once been the ravishing Lady Susan Glanville.

The creature reeled back with an agonized scream which drowned out the cries of the Earl. It cowered on the bench, abruptly silent and motionless, only the pulsating of its wizened mouth and the fires of hatred in its red eyes giving evidence that it still lived.

William Cowath addressed it grimly. "Creature of

hell! If ye leave that bench ere we quit this room and seal it once again, I swear that I shall hold this cross against ye!''

The thing's red eyes watched the Factor with an expression of abysmal hatred. They actually appeared to glow with fire. And yet I read in them something else—fear.

I suddenly became aware that silence had descended on that room of the damned. It lasted only a few moments. The Earl had finally stopped screaming, but now came something worse. He began to laugh.

It was only a low chuckle, but it was somehow worse than all his screams. It went on and on, softly, mindlessly.

The Factor turned, beckoning me toward the partially demolished wall. Crossing the room, I climbed out. Behind me the Factor led the young Earl, who shuffled like an old man, chuckling to himself.

There was then what seemed an interminable interval, during which the Factor carried back a sack of mortar and a keg of water which he had previously left somewhere in the tunnel. Working by torchlight, he prepared the cement and proceeded to seal up the chamber, using the same stones which he had displaced.

While the Factor labored, the young Earl sat motionless in the tunnel, chuckling softly.

There was silence from within. Once, only, I heard the thing's fetters clank against stone.

At last the Factor finished and led us back through those nitre-stained passageways and up the icy stairs. The Earl could scarcely ascend; with difficulty the Factor supported him from step to step.

Back in his tapestry-panelled chamber, Earl Frederick sat on his canopy bed and stared at the floor, laughing quietly. Medical tomes to the contrary, I noticed that his black hair had actually turned gray. After persuading him to drink a glass of liquid which I had no doubt contained a heavy dose of sedation, the Factor managed to get him stretched out on the bed.

William Cowath then led me to a nearby bed chamber. My impulse was to rush from that hellish pile without delay, but the storm still raged and I was by no means sure I could find my way back to the village without a guide.

The Factor shook his head sadly. "I fear his Lordship is doomed to an early death. He was never strong and tonight's events may have deranged his mind—may have weakened him beyond hope of recovery."

I expressed my sympathy and horror. The Factor's cold blue eyes held my own. "It may be," he said, "that in the event of the young Earl's death, you yourself might be considered . . . ." He hesitated. "Might be considered," he finally concluded, "as one somewhat in the line of succession."

I wanted to hear no more. I gave him a curt goodnight, bolted the door after him and tried—quite unsuccessfully—to salvage a few minutes' sleep.

But sleep would not come. I had feverish visions of that red-eyed thing in the sealed chamber escaping its fetters, breaking through the wall and crawling up those icy, slime-covered stairs . . . .

Even before dawn I softly unbolted my door and like a marauding thief crept shivering through the cold passageways and the great deserted hall of the castle. Crossing the cobbled courtyards and the black moat, I scrambled down the incline toward the village.

Long before noon I was well on my way to London. Luck was with me; the next day I was on a boat bound for the Altantic run.

I shall never return to England. I intend always to keep Chilton Castle and its permanent occupant at least an ocean away.

The
Impulse
to Kill

The desire, the urge, the impulse to kill is in all of us. It is as old as life itself. Nothing fills us with a greater sense of power, of exhilaration, than killing. Nothing affords a more intense excitement or a greater release of pent-up tension.

Our remote ancestors killed for survival, for the warmest cave, the richest game area, the most desirable mate. Our more immediate forebears killed for power, for conquest, for sport. The age-old impulse is deeply planted.

In former times wars afforded a vast measure of relief. What secret rejoicings there were when war was declared. To be able to kill again without penalty! To kill and be proclaimed a hero! Nearly all countries, sooner or later, resorted to war. Their leaders knew it was a sure way to relieve internal pressures, to siphon off dangerous energy and impulses.

Now, unfortunately, war has become impersonal, dehumanized. There is little personal killing. It has become remote, wholesale, a matter of massive bombs, unseen missiles, gases, pushbuttons. Science has spoiled one of our international pastimes.

But the impulse to kill, to kill directly and in person, remains. Witness the daily headlines — the slashings and shootings, the lethal beatings, the endless round of hourly murder. The killing instinct, obviously, remains strong in us, even in spite of the penalties which may be meted out.

Since my early youth I myself have experienced an impulse to kill. Although a fine inheritance endowed me with the means for education, travel, and endless entertainment, eventually everything began to seem boring. Food and drink, women, gambling, study and philosophical speculation, even work—all became tedious, meaningless.

I knew of course, all along, what my secret desire really was, but I was afraid to face up to it. I was afraid of myself; I was afraid of the penalties; I was afraid of being afraid. Finally, one night, I reached such a state of abysmal boredom and depression that I contemplated suicide. But at the last moment I rebelled.

I reasoned: why destroy myself, cultured, experienced, and intelligent as I was, when there were so many thousands of clods and fools whose dull shabby lives could have no meaning for themselves or for anyone else?—so many half-witted specimens who contributed nothing to anyone, whose mere existence created a burden for someone?

Once I had made my resolution, only one problem remained—the penalties. I certainly had no intention of being electrocuted or gassed in exchange for the demise of some idiot who was not worth a snap of my fingers.

The problem remained unsolved for some time and the solution came about by accident.

Traveling around as always, I happened to be in a

small town in Illinois. I had a hotel room, and I was walking around the town one summer evening, hoping to find amusement. I had fully determined to kill at this point, but the means I would employ still eluded me.

As I walked, I grew thirsty; I stopped in at a neighborhood bar and ordered beer. It was a typical, dismal, raucous little dive complete with juke box, television, and the local loudmouth who had had too many drinks.

As it happened, I had no change, so I took out my wallet when the beer arrived. The wallet was solidly packed with bills. As I slipped out a dollar, I noticed a number of the bar sops eying the wallet with keen interest. That gave me an idea.

I finished my beer and then went back to my hotel room to think. Long before I went to bed, my plans were made.

In less than three weeks I was living in a small furnished house on the outskirts of that town.

Once I got settled, I began taking daily walks. After strolling around the central shopping district, I would stop in at the little neighborhood bar—the Cameo—where I had got my idea. I usually ordered beer, but more often than not I paid for my drinks with folding money. My wallet, bulky with bills, was much in evidence.

I began casual conversations with some of the habitués. I explained, honestly enough, that I was retired on the income from a family trust. I was rather vague about my reasons for staying in the town. I just said that I had grown tired of big-city life and that I liked the slower pace of a small town.

After some time I rated surface cordiality, but I knew that I remained an object of envy and suspicion. That suited me fine; I didn't want to become too well liked. So long as I could hold casual conversations with the bar trade and flash my roll around, my plans were working smoothly.

One afternoon when I walked into the Cameo, nearly everyone was talking about the terrific thunder shower of the night before. It was one of the worst I had ever experienced; it had kept me awake for hours.

But I pretended surprise as I listened to comments about the storm. I insisted that I hadn't heard a thing. I had slept, I announced, right through till dawn without a break. By way of explanation, I added that I was a very sound sleeper and that ordinarily nothing short of an earthquake or a tornado would wake me up.

As I made this statement, I noticed several of the bar sops watching me with renewed interest. They were the very ones who usually kept their eyes glued to my wallet when I paid for my drinks. One of them in particular attracted my attention.

His name was Frank Reffalto. He was a wiry, dark, sharp-featured young punk who made occasional trips to Chicago and who seemed to manage without working. I wasn't sure, of course, but I decided right there that he was probably the one.

That very night I changed my sleeping schedule. It wasn't hard for me. Actually, instead of being a sound sleeper, I am an insomniac. It takes me hours to get to sleep. I can stay awake all night with little effort. Now it was extra easy.

By ten o'clock all the lights in my house were out —but I was wide awake. I had a flashlight handy and a loaded .38 revolver tucked in my belt. I sat quietly while my eyes adjusted to the darkness. Every hour or so I made a round of the house, moving carefully and keeping back from the windows.

Nothing happened that night. When the sun began coming up, I went to bed. I slept nearly five hours and woke up perfectly refreshed.

That afternoon I was back in the Cameo bar,

flashing my roll of bills, boasting what a sound sleeper I was. I exchanged pleasantries with Frank Reffalto. He was unusually genial; we wound up buying each other drinks.

I continued my nightly watch. The almost unbearable tensions building up in me were a little soothed by my solitary vigil. I liked the darkness, the quietness, the sense of expectancy. And the new sleeping schedule all but cured my insomnia. By dawn I was tired but relaxed; I could sleep my necessary four or five hours.

One night, after I had been on my night schedule for about two weeks, I felt unusually tense and expectant. Maybe it was just the full moon—or maybe I'm actually telepathic as I have always believed.

I prowled the house every half hour, watching, listening. With the aid of the moonlight, I could see perfectly. And my hearing had grown more acute after hours of nighttime listening. I could hear every small rustle, every tiny click and crepitation.

It was a lovely night. Moonlight turned the earth to an immense silver shield. My solitary house, set apart in its little plot, was like the secret home of a magician where anything might happen.

I heard someone walking softly outside. I was alert and ready in an instant. My heart beat wildly with joy rather than fear.

Concealing myself in a dark corner of the living room behind a window drape, I waited hopefully, the .38 in my hand with the safety off.

A board on the back porch creaked, and then there was a fumbling at a window. I heard the tinkle of falling glass, the sound of a window being slowly raised.

While one hand held the .38, I reached for the light switch with the other.

My bedroom was upstairs. A prowler entering through the porch window would have to cross through the kitchen and into the living room to reach the foot of the stairs.

The beam of a tiny flashlight stabbed the darkness. Someone stumbled against a chair in the kitchen, swore softly. The flashlight beam danced forward into the living room.

When the intruder was halfway across the room, I flipped the light switch. There was plenty of moonlight; I could have managed without the electric. But I didn't want to miss any small part of this special midnight performance. I had waited too long for that.

It was Frank Reffalto. He stood there with such a stupefied, comical look on his face that I almost laughed. How I savored the moment! The burst of light all but blinded him. He looked around wildly without seeing me.

Aiming for the belly, I fired carefully. Frank Reffalto screamed, dropped the flashlight and doubled over, grabbing at his guts. He teetered there in the middle of the room, doing a crazy lurching little dance while his face turned green and greasy.

I called softly, "Frank!" He looked up and saw me. Smiling at him, I fired again. This one caught him in the chest, and he toppled over backwards.

He twitched and kicked a few times and lay still.

Sighing, I stepped out from behind the drapes. I was sorry it was over so soon, but I was filled with a wonderful sense of peace, of accomplishment. All the dark, knotted tensions melted away. I felt more relaxed and satisfied than I had ever been in my life. A feeling of power, of soaring exhilaration, surged through me like a rare and cherished wine. At last I had found a way to accomodate the lethal impulse which had tormented me for years!

Patting Frank Reffalto's pockets, I found a small automatic. Taking it our with my handkerchief, I pressed it into his hand. Then I called the police.

There was never any question about the killing. The investigation was purely routine. I told the police that after I heard a noise, I got out of bed, took my gun from a drawer, and came downstairs. I said that I met Frank Reffalto in the living room, that I saw the moonlight glinting on the automatic in his hand. I fired. What else could I have done? Under the circumstances it was sheer self-defense.

Also, as I suspected, Frank Reffalto had a police record. He had been arrested for burglary in Chicago and had spent some time in jail.

I had done society a service. Who would ever believe that I had deliberately lured Frank Reffalto to his death?

I didn't depart immediately; that might create suspicion. But I remained away from the Cameo bar, and after a few weeks I left town unobtrusively. The climate in that town had become, I felt, a trifle unhealthful. I didn't fear the police, but I couldn't be sure that Frank Reffalto's friends might not resent the manner of his passing.

I drove around aimlessly for a few weeks, finally settling in a small town in southern California. For a time I was content to loaf. I went swimming, read quietly in my hotel room—and reminisced. I was completely relaxed and serene. In my own mind I reenacted the killing of Frank Reffalto a hundred times. The memory of it soothed and amused me.

But, gradually, the past began to pall. Slowly the old tension built up again. I became restless and irritable. I didn't try to fight off the impulse. I knew what I had to do.

I rented a little house near the outskirts of town. Shortly after that I began visiting a neighborhood bar. My billfold, firmly packed, was much in evidence. Before long I was telling the local bar sops what a sound sleeper I was.

It worked like magic. A few weeks after I began

stopping in at the bar, I looked out of my window one evening and saw someone standing across the street, studying the house. I thought I recognized the young punk, but I wasn't sure.

That very night all my lights went out at ten, and I began my vigil. I padded around the house like a great cat, hungry, silent, waiting to kill. During the day I was all knotted up with tension, but at night I relaxed a little. I prowled patiently, alert to every sound, every shadow.

The break came sooner than I had expected. I was standing in the darkness one midnight, looking out my bedroom window, when I heard someone trying the rear screen door. Only a small catch lock kept it secured.

I tensed as I heard the lock wrenched out. My visitor had no light, but I could see so well in the dark it didn't matter. When he came into the bedroom, I was hunched in a dark corner, .38 held ready.

I let him cross to the middle of the room where he made a perfect target. He paused there, never knowing he was an instant away from oblivion. How I relished that moment! I felt a surge of wild, primitive joy. The age-old killer instinct coursed through me like a flame, searing away everything else.

Aiming very carefully, I fired at his belt line. He sagged down with scarcely a sound and just lay there. He was so silent, I grew a little suspicious. Just to make sure I fired twice more. Both slugs ripped into him, and he didn't move.

I was coming out of the corner when I heard the sound of running feet.

I didn't think; I acted. I was out the rear door like a tiger bounding after his prey.

Someone was running across the field in the back, making toward a fringe of trees. I fired twice as I ran and somebody yelled.

Then he was down there in the burdock weeds and the burnt grass, his strained white face watching anxiously as I circled warily at a distance.

"Have you got a gun?" I asked.

He sounded like a kid who'd got stung by a bee. "No," he said. "I got no gun."

I waited a moment and a rush of words came out of him, panic changing his voice. "I'm bleedin' bad, Mac. My leg. Get a doctor. Hurry up, get a doctor, Mac!"

Grinning, I moved up on him. His mouth fell open; his eyes looked as if they'd saucer right out of his head.

I inched closer, making sure of my aim. I would have waited longer, but a kind of shocked, sudden understanding hit him. He closed his mouth. When he opened it again, I figured he'd start yelling for help.

The slug caught him right between the eyes. He slammed over on his back and lay there motionless in the grass with one leg twisted underneath him at a crazy angle.

After that people came running, including the cops. I was commended for the thorough job I'd done.

But later on I was called in for a few questions. The punk I'd killed inside the house had a gun. But the police were a bit uneasy about the young thug I'd shot in the back field. Apparently he had acted as lookout. But he wasn't armed. And the police had figured out that he was shot in the head after he was shot in the leg.

I explained that I thought he might be faking, that I'd seen him reach into a pocket for what I assumed was a gun.

"Probably getting his handkerchief to use as a tourniquet," one of the detectives suggested.

I shrugged. "That might be," I acknowledged, "but how was I to know?"

That ended the interview. I was dismissed and never called back. If there was any lingering sympathy for the young punks I'd killed, it was pretty much diluted a few days later when a local housewife was stabbed to death by a burglar who got away.

After a decent interval, I left town. I was relaxed, loose, and easy again. I drove towards the East Coast at a leisurely pace. I was content to roll along and look at the scenery. At night I'd stop in a motel and watch television. Sometimes I'd spend long periods just lying back on the bed, thinking about those two suckers I'd killed in California. In my mind I killed them over and over again. It was great fun; it helped hold off my insomnia.

I reached New York and managed to find entertainment for a while. But after a couple of months, I began to get bored. I grew less relaxed as each day passed. My insomnia came back; I found myself getting moody and irritable.

Finally I could stand it no longer. I drove up to Connecticut and looked around. I knew what I was going to do, and I went at it with great deliberation.

I settled in a little town and rented a cottage near the outskirts. I've already been visiting the local bar. I carry a thick roll of bills, and I never seem to have any change when I buy drinks.

Lately I've been bragging about how only a dynamite blast can wake me up once I get to sleep. The bar sops have taken a definite interest in me.

One of these nights somebody will be around to pay me an unscheduled visit.

I can hardly wait . . . .

The House on Hazel Street

That hot dry summer I was nearly penniless. I roamed the gritty streets simply to get out of the insufferable cage which had been advertised as "an airy furnished room." Going from my cubicle to the street was like stepping from a furnace into an oven, but at least there was some degree of difference. I wandered restlessly, weak with the heat and yet too fretful to sit still. I had thought I was familiar with New Haven, but I perspired down streets I had never heard of before. I walked endlessly.

That was the way I discovered the blistered house on Hazel Street. It was set back a bit from its teeming, dilapidated neighbors, shuttered, silent, warped, and secret. Its gray paint had cracked and peeled away, leaving it dingy and mottled. The first time I saw it I experienced an eerie feeling that somehow it stood apart in time, that it was simply the ghost of something else, the visible yet deceptive shell of another structure. But I was overheated to the point of collapse, and near delirium produces strange effects.

That evening as I lay on my lumpy cot in Mrs. Fern's suffocating "airy" room, the house kept appearing in my mind. Wearily I told myself that it was nothing but a simple wooden frame house, tenantless, neglected by its owner, left to decay on a dingy street near a waterfront slum where once—eighty years ago—there may have been a flourishing stand of hazel trees.

But it wouldn't do. The next day I was back on Hazel Street, squinting at the infernal rattrap. The street shimmered in the heat; even the screeching urchins and the snarling little dogs were inactive for once. I stood surveying the house at leisure, oblivious to the sweat runnelling my seedy clothes.

And then the door opened. I didn't see it move, but suddenly it was open. There in the dim shadows someone beckoned.

I had no desire to go in—yet I did. I walked up a moss-chinked brick path, past a front yard overgrown with dead rose bushes, and climbed a short flight of creaky wooden stairs. Just inside the door stood a little old man who looked as if he had crawled out from under the eaves after hibernating for half a century. He was so bent and old I wondered that he hung together. His threadbare brown suit looked like so much accumulated rust which had been thrown at him in handfulls. Some had adhered and that was the suit.

But I went in anyway and soon found myself sitting in a dark, cobwebbed parlour filled with huge portraits, big Victorian chairs covered with antimacassars, and all manner of bric-a-brac drowning in dust.

My elfish host hovered in the shadows, bowing, clasping his castanet hands. "I observed you watching the house. I knew you were intrigued. So I have asked you in! Would you care for a drink of sarsaparilla?''

At that moment I could have drunk boiled ditch water. I nodded an affirmative.

While I toyed with a cut-glass cup (I drank the sarsaparilla in a gulp) my host introduced himself. "I am Jonathan Sellerby," he said. "I have lived in this house for ninety-seven years. I was born here."

I looked at him in surprise. One rarely meets a ninety-seven year-old who is not confined to bed or a wheel chair.

His colorless eyes held my own. "Ninety-seven years. But what is that? What is time? A pile of years like so many bricks? Little slices of life all stacked together? How silly we are! Time is a dimension. Time is eternal."

The intensity and earnestness of his speech startled me. But then I reflected that he had probably been living alone for years. Brooding by himself, he had acquired strange ideas. At least he appeared harmless.

"More sarsaparilla?" I handed him my glass. While he tottered out, I inspected the room, but it was so dark inside with the shutters drawn I could make out few details. The furnishings were uniformly Victorian—massive, ornate chairs and "settles," fringed hangings, an old foot-pump organ, all coated with a deep layer of gray dust.

My host handed me the second cup of sarsaparilla with a courtly bow. "It isn't what it used to be—what it was when I was a young man. It had taste then. Why that was the big event of the week. On Saturday night we'd go over to Turner's Emporium and order sarsaparilla! I tell you it was something to drink in those days!"

A peculiar look came into his eyes, and he fairly shook with excitement. "Maybe—maybe tonight we can go over! Just the two of us. It's right across the street on the corner. We'll wait till the gas lamps are lit and most of the brewery wagons are off the street, and then we'll run over there for a real glass . . . ." He stared at me. "What is it, sir? Are you ill?"

I don't know what it was—his crazy rambling, the heat, the musty air of the room—but suddenly I tried to get up and I felt dizzy and weak as an infant. Sinking back in my chair, I shook my head. "Just a dizzy spell. Be fine in a minute."

But I wasn't. Although I didn't feel sick, I remained weak and giddy. The thought of going back out into the blazing heat of the pavements appalled me.

My host, Jonathan Sellerby, sensed my apprehension. His gnomish wrinkled face showed genuine solicitude. He nodded nimbly. "You are welcome to remain," he said. "Tonight it will be cooler. You'll see. And now, if you will excuse me . . . ."

As he left the room, I closed my eyes and settled back in my chair. It was an odd business certainly, but I assured myself that the sensible thing to do was regain my strength before I ventured onto the streets.

As I half dozed, I wondered why I had come into the house in the first place. What had prompted me? It was absurd, now that I thought about it. Old Mr. Sellerby had simply opened the door and beckoned, and I had walked in. How completely ridiculous! But after all, I told myself, the house *had* fascinated me. Something about it attracted my attention certainly, so it was only natural that I should come in to see Mr. Sellerby, to help Mr. Sellerby go back wherever he was going, where he and I were going, going together tonight. Where were we going? Of course I knew. We were—going—I almost had it then—yes! yes! yes! We were going to Turner's Emporium for sarsaparilla! The kind of sarsaparilla they didn't make any more. That old-time flavor.

I sat up suddenly. Where was Mr. Sellerby?

He came softly into the room, his eyes intent upon my own, his finger on his lips. I could hear every syllable he said, and yet it seemed as if his mouth formed words without making any sound.

He smiled encouragingly. "It is just a bit too early, too soon, sir. Time is turning back, but it is slow, slow. Now I'm going out to the carriage shed in back. The old things are strong there, friend! You can smell the horses, the harnesses, sweet hay in the stalls—the very dust. It will all come back soon. You must be patient. It only takes enough will, enough purpose—enough longing! Patience. Patience."

Fear inched its way along my spine as he hurried out of the room. He was mad, certainly, and I had better get out of there. But when I moved, I felt helpless. Every last reserve of strength seemed to have ebbed out of me.

Then I began thinking about Turner's Emporium again, and I really didn't care. It *would* be fun to go over for a sarsaparilla. We'd sit on those little wire chairs at a marble-topped table and sip the most delicious sarsaparilla that ever was made. We'd be part of Saturday night. Gem Jackson and the boys would be down on the corner singing, and there'd be the rustle of starched skirts along the brick sidewalks. They might even have fireworks somewhere and maybe—

I fell asleep. At least I remembered nothing more until Mr. Sellerby stole quietly into the room and shook my shoulder. I woke up abruptly, forgetting for the moment where I was. And then I gazed around the room in amazement.

The dust was gone. A gas light flickered on one wall; in its soft glow everything looked polished and new. The chairs seemed to have been recently upholstered, and the gilded portraits gleamed. The rug, before nothing but a sort of gray smudge, now revealed a colorful flower pattern of pink and blue. I rubbed my eyes and looked again; the transformation remained.

I stared at Mr. Sellerby. "You've—cleaned the room?"

He smiled gently, shaking his head. "Go to the window and look out."

As I arose, I noticed that his decrepit brown suit had been replaced by a new one which was creased and spotless. He wore a brown bowler hat and jauntily swung a gold-headed walking stick.

Still feeling weak, I walked to the window. The shutters had been opened. Pulling a fringed brocade curtain aside, I looked out.

I gasped. The entire street seemed changed. Gas lamps flared on iron posts. The wide macadam of the roadway was now a narrow strip of cobblestones; the asphalt pavements were red brick. As I watched in disbelief, a big brewery wagon laden with wooden kegs rumbled past on the cobbles.

Mr. Sellerby was at my side, pointing toward the corner. "Look there," he said.

On the corner, diagonally across the cobblestone street, was a brightly illuminated store. I read the ornate lettering on the plate-glass window: "Turner's Emporium—Lemon Ice—Sarsaparilla—All Soda Flavors."

Mr. Sellerby took my arm. "Come. We will go over together!"

I felt helpless, as if I had no will of my own. Turning from the window, I followed him toward the door. We stepped outside into the soft air of early summer. The scent of roses came to me, and as we walked down the brick path toward the street, I saw that the front yard was a mass of blooming rose bushes.

Mr. Sellerby began humming to himself an old melody which I had seen once in a tattered song book. I couldn't remember the title but one line went: "In the moonlight, darling, you and I will vow."

Somewhere in the distance I heard mingled voices harmonizing. They were off-key, even harsh, yet for some reason peculiarly nostalgic, strangely evocative. I paused to listen.

Mr. Sellerby smiled up at me. "That will be Gem Jackson and some of the brewery boys. A bit rusty now—out of practice—but wait till later on in the summer. You'll be willing to stand and listen to them all night long!"

As we reached the brick sidewalk, a wave of dizziness swept over me. Somewhere, deep within my subconscious, in my very marrow, a warning flashed. I *knew*—without thinking, without reasoning—that once I crossed that cobblestone street and entered Turner's Emporium, I would never come back. The realization of this filled me with sudden uncontrollable panic, with a terror beyond argument. Shaking off Mr. Sellerby's arm, I whirled and ran back up the path, up the steps to the door. As I pulled it open, I looked, once, over my shoulder.

Mr. Sellerby had turned and was staring at me with astonishment. Finally he shrugged and shook his head. Then a look of inexpressible happiness, of beatific anticipation, changed his face. Swinging his ebony cane, he turned and started across the cobblestone street toward Turner's Emporium.

Slamming the door behind me, I rushed inside, collapsed in a chair, and closed my eyes. My brain, or some vital part of my being, seemed to be swimming through a humming sea of space. I think of the word "vertigo" and yet that scarcely expresses what I experienced. I felt disembodied, lost in some nameless dimension over which I had no control. Far, far away, far in infinite distance, I could still hear the faint sound of singing, off-key, yet haunting, compelling. Finally this faded, and at last oblivion swept over me.

It was early morning when I awoke in the same dusty, shuttered room of the afternoon before. Jonathan Sellerby was nowhere in sight. On a nearby table I saw a cut-glass cup and the ring made by its wet base. I got up, giddily, and walked to the door. I called but there was no reply.

As I walked down the brick path, I saw that the front yard was a black tangle of dead rose bushes. The heat had abated somewhat, and I made my way back to my room without incident.

Of course that wasn't the end of it. In a few days the police arrived. Jonathan Sellerby had disappeared, and I had been seen emerging from his house. What had I done with his body?

I told them, quite truthfully, that he had gone out the evening prior to my departure and never returned. Hours of grilling got nothing more out of me. I was arrested, released, rearrested, and eventually turned loose again with a sullen promise that the case would not be closed.

My own theory is that Jonathan Sellerby sat alone in that shadowy, shuttered house for a half century or more, longing with terrible intensity for the past, for the happy days of his early youth. I think, at the climax, he may have used my own brain, intentionally or perhaps only accidentally, as a sort of battery or charging unit to strengthen the unceasing waves of his desire. And again, perhaps accidentally—it worked. His ever-present memories of the past, his intense visualizations, his precise recollections of sights and sounds and smells, finally resurrected a period which had passed but which still existed somewhere in the flowing dimension of time.

But how could I tell the police they could find him in Turner's Emporium, sipping sarsaparilla, back around 1890?

Slime

It was a great gray-black hood of horror moving over the floor of the sea. It slid through the soft ooze like a monstrous mantle of slime obscenely animated with questing life. It was by turns viscid and fluid. At times it flattened out and flowed through the carpet of mud like an inky pool; occasionally it paused, seeming to shrink in upon itself, then reared up out of the ooze until it resembled an irregular cone or a gigantic hood. Although it possessed no eyes, it had a marvelously developed sense of touch, and it possessed a sensitivity to minute vibrations which was almost akin to telepathy. It was plastic, essentially shapeless. It could shoot out long tentacles until it bore a resemblance to a nightmare squid or a huge starfish; it could retract itself into a round flattened disk or squeeze into an irregular hunched shape so that it looked like a black boulder sunk on the bottom of the sea.

It had prowled the black water endlessly. It had been formed when the earth and the seas were young;

it was almost as old as the ocean itself. It moved through a night which had no beginning and no dissolution. The black sea basin where it lurked had been dark since the world began—an environment only a little less inimical than the stupendous gulfs of interplanetary space.

It was animated by a single, unceasing, never-satisfied drive: a voracious, insatiable hunger. It could survive for months without food, but minutes after eating it was as ravenous as ever. Its appetite was appalling and incalculable.

On the icy ink-black floor of the sea the battle for survival was savage, hideous—and usually brief. But for the shape there was no battle. It ate whatever came its way, regardless of size or disposition. It absorbed microscopic plankton and giant squid with equal assurance. Had its surface been less fluid, it might have retained the circular scars left by the grappling suckers of the wildly threshing deep-water squid or the jagged toothmarks of the anachronistic frillshark, but as it was, neither left any evidence of its absorption. When the lifting curtain of living slime swayed out of the mud and closed upon them, their fiercest death throes came to nothing.

The horror did not know fear. There was nothing to be afraid of. It ate whatever moved or tried not to move, and it had never encountered anything which could, in turn, eat it. If a squid's sucker or a shark's tooth tore into the mass of its viscosity, the rent flowed in upon itself and immediately closed. If a segment was detached, it could be retrieved and absorbed back into the whole.

The black mantle reigned supreme in its savage world of slime and silence. It groped greedily and endlessly through the mud, eating and never sleeping, never resting. If it lay still, it was only to trap food which might otherwise be lost. If it rushed with terrifying speed across the slimy bottom, it was never to escape an enemy, but always to flop its hideous fluidity upon its sole and inevitable quarry—food.

It had evolved out of the muck and slime of the primitive sea floor, and it was as alien to ordinary terrestrial life as the weird denizens of some wild planet in a distant galaxy. It was an experiment of nature compared to which the saber-toothed tiger; the wooly mammoth and even Tyrannosaurus, the slashing, murderous king of the great earth reptiles, were as tame, weak entities.

Had it not been for a vast volcanic upheaval on the bottom of the ocean basin, the black horror would have crept out its entire existence on the silent sea ooze without ever manifesting its hideous powers to mankind.

Fate, in the form of a violent subterranean explosion, covering huge areas of the ocean's floor, hurled it out of its black slime world and sent it spinning toward the surface.

Had it been an ordinary deep-water fish, it never would have survived the experience. The explosion itself, or the drastic lessening of water pressure as it shot toward the surface, would have destroyed it. But it was no ordinary fish. Its viscosity or plasticity or whatever it was that constituted its essentially amoebic structure, permitted it to survive.

It reached the surface slightly stunned and flopped on the surging waters like a great blob of black blubber. Immense waves stirred up by the subterranean explosion swept it swiftly toward shore, and because it was somewhat stunned it did not try to resist the roaring mountains of water.

Along with scattered ash, pumice, and the puffed bodies of dead fish, the black horror was hurled toward a beach. The huge waves carried it more than a mile inland, far beyond the strip of sandy shore, and deposited it in the midst of a deep, brackish swamp area.

As luck would have it, the submarine explosion

and subsequent tidal wave took place at night, and therefore the slime horror was not immediately subjected to a new and hateful experience—light.

Although the midnight darkness of the storm-lashed swamp did not begin to compare with the stygian blackness of the sea bottom where even violet rays of the spectrum could not penetrate, the marsh darkness was nevertheless deep and intense.

As the water of the great wave receded, sluicing through the thorn jungle and back out to sea, the black horror clung to a mud bank surrounded by a rank growth of cattails. It was aware of the sudden, startling change in its environment; and for some time it lay motionless, concentrating its attention on obscure internal readjustment which the absence of crushing pressure and a surrounding cloak of frigid sea water demanded. Its adaptability was incredible. It achieved in a few hours what an ordinary creature could have attained only through a process of gradual evolution. Three hours after the titanic wave flopped it onto the mud bank, it had undergone swift organic changes which left it relatively at ease in its new environment.

In fact, it felt lighter and more mobile than it ever had before in its sea basin existence.

As it flung out feelers and attuned itself to the minutest vibrations and emanations of the swamp area, its pristine hunger drive reasserted itself with overwhelming urgency. And the tale which its sensory apparatus returned to the monstrous something which served it as a brain, excited it tremendously. It sensed at once that the swamp was filled with luscious tidbits of quivering food—more food and food of a greater variety than it had ever encountered on the cold floor of the sea.

Its savage, incessant hunger seemed unbearable. Its slimy mass was swept by a shuddering wave of anticipation.

Sliding off the mud bank, it slithered over the cattails into an adjacent area consisting of deep black pools interspersed with water-logged tussocks. Weed stalks stuck up out of the water, and the decayed trunks of fallen trees floated half-submerged in the larger pools.

Ravenous with hunger, it sloshed into the bog area, flicking its fluid tentacles about. Within minutes it had snatched up several fat frogs and a number of small fish. These, however, merely titillated its appetite. Its hunger turned into a kind of ecstatic fury. It commenced a systematic hunt, plunging to the bottom of each pool and quickly but carefully exploring every inch of its oozy bottom. The first creature of any size which it encountered was a muskrat. An immense curtain of adhesive slime suddenly swept out of the darkness, closed upon it—and squeezed.

Heartened and whetted by its find, the hood of horror rummaged the rank pools with renewed zeal. When it surfaced, it carefully probed the tussocks for anything that might have escaped it in the water. Once it snatched up a small bird nesting in some swamp grass. Occasionally it slithered up the crisscrossed trunks of fallen trees, bearing them down with its unspeakable slimy bulk, and hung briefly suspended like a great dripping curtain of black marsh mud.

It was approaching a somewhat less swampy and more deeply wooded area when it gradually became aware of a subtle change in its new environment. It paused, hesitating, and remained half in and half out of a small pond near the edge of the nearest trees.

Although it had absorbed twenty-five or thirty pounds of food in the form of frogs, fish, water snakes, the muskrat, and a few smaller creatures, its fierce hunger had not left it. Its monstrous appetite urged it on, and yet something held it anchored in the pond.

What it sensed, but could not literally see, was the

rising sun spreading a gray light over the swamp. The horror had never encountered any illumination except that generated by the grotesque phosphorescent appendages of various deep-sea fishes. Natural light was totally unknown to it.

As the dawn light strengthened, breaking through the scattering storm clouds, the black slime monster fresh from the inky floor of the sea sensed that something utterly unknown was flooding in upon it. Light was hateful to it. It cast out quick feelers, hoping to catch and crush the light. But the more frenzied its efforts became, the more intense became the abhorred aura surrounding it.

At length, as the sun rose visibly above the trees, the horror, in baffled rage rather than in fear, grudgingly slid back into the pond and burrowed into the soft ooze of its bottom. There it remained while the sun shone and the small creatures of the swamp ventured forth on furtive errands.

A few miles away from Wharton's Swamp, in the small town of Clinton Center, Henry Hossing sleepily crawled out of the improvised shack in an alley which had afforded him a degree of shelter for the night and stumbled into the street. Passing a hand across his rheumy eyes, he scratched the stubble on his cheek and blinked listlessly at the rising sun. He had not slept well; the storm of the night before had kept him awake. Besides he had gone to bed hungry, and that never agreed with him.

Glancing furtively along the street, he walked slouched forward with his head bent down. Most of the time he kept his eyes on the walk or on the gutter in the hopes of spotting a chance coin.

Clinton Center had not been kind to him. The handouts were sparse, and only yesterday he had been warned out of town by one of the local policemen.

Grumbling to himself, he reached the end of the street and started to cross. Suddenly he stopped quickly and snatched up something from the edge of the pavement.

It was a crumpled green bill, and as he frantically unfolded it, a look of stupefied rapture spread across his bristly face. Ten dollars! More money than he had possessed at any one time in months.

Stowing it carefully in the one good pocket of his seedy gray jacket, he crossed the street with a swift stride. Instead of sweeping the sidewalks, his eyes now darted along the rows of stores and restaurants.

He paused at one restaurant, hesitated, and finally went on until he found another less pretentious one a few blocks away.

When he sat down, the counterman shook his head. "Get goin', bud. No free coffee today."

With a wide grin, the hobo produced his ten-dollar bill and spread it on the counter. "That covers a good breakfast here, pardner?"

The counterman seemed irritated. "O.K. O.K. What'll you have?" He eyed the bill suspiciously.

Henry Hossing ordered orange juice, toast, ham and eggs, oatmeal, melon, and coffee.

When it appeared, he ate every bit of it, ordered three additional cups of coffee, paid the check as if two-dollar breakfasts were customary with him, and then sauntered back to the street.

Shortly after noon, after his three-dollar lunch, he saw the liquor store. For a few minutes he stood across the street from it, fingering his five-dollar bill. Finally he crossed with an abstracted smile, entered, and bought a quart of rye.

He hesitated on the sidewalk, debating whether or not he should return to the little shack in the side alley. After a minute or two of indecision, he decided against it and struck out instead for Wharton's Swamp. The local police were far less likely to disturb him there, and since the skies were clearing and the weather mild, there was little immediate need of shelter.

Angling off the highway which skirted the swamp several miles from town, he crossed a marshy meadow, pushed through a fringe of brush, and sat down under a sweet-gum tree which bordered a deeply wooded area.

By late afternoon he had achieved a quite cheerful glow, and he had little inclination to return to Clinton Center. Rousing himself from reverie, he stumbled about collecting enough wood for a small fire and went back to his sylvan seat under the sweet gum.

He slept briefly as dusk descended, but finally bestirred himself again to build a fire, as deeper shadows fell over the swamp. Then he returned to his swiftly diminishing bottle.

He was suspended in a warm net of inflamed fantasy when something abruptly broke the spell and brought him back to earth.

The flickering flames of his fire had dwindled down until now only a dim eerie glow illuminated the immediate area under the sweet gum. He saw nothing and at the moment heard nothing, and yet he was filled with a sudden and profound sense of lurking menace.

He stood up, staggering, leaned back against the sweet gum, and peered fearfully into the shadows. In the deep darkness beyond the waning arc of firelight, he could distinguish nothing which had any discernible form or color.

Then he detected the stench and shuddered. In spite of the reek of cheap whiskey which clung around him, the smell was overpowering. It was a heavy, fulsome fetor, alien and utterly repellent. It was vaguely fish-like, but otherwise beyond any known comparison.

As he stood trembling under the sweet gum, Henry Hossing thought of something dead which had lain for long ages at the bottom of the sea.

Filled with mounting alarm, he looked around for some wood which he might add to the dying fire. All he could find nearby however were a few twigs. He threw these on, and the flames licked up briefly and subsided.

He listened and heard—or imagined he heard—an odd sort of slithering sound in the nearby bushes. It seemed to retreat slightly as the flames shot up.

Genuine terror took possession of him. He knew that he was in no condition to flee—and now he came to the horrifying conclusion that, whatever unspeakable menace waited in the surrounding darkness, it was temporarily held at bay only by the failing gleam of his little fire.

Frantically he looked around for more wood. But there was none. None, that is, within the faint glow of firelight. And he dared not venture beyond.

He began to tremble uncontrollably. He tried to scream, but no sound came out of tightened throat.

The ghastly stench became stronger, and now he was sure that he could hear a strange sliding, slithering sound in the black shadows beyond the remaining spark of firelight.

He stood frozen in absolute helpless panic as the tiny fire smouldered down into darkness.

At the last instant a charred bit of wood broke apart, sending up a few sparks, and in that flicker of final light he glimpsed the horror.

It had already glided out of the bushes, and now it rushed across the small clearing with nightmare speed. It was a final incarnation of all the fears, shuddering apprehensions, and bad dreams which Henry Hossing had ever known in his life. It was a fiend from the pit of Hell come to claim him at last.

A terrible ringing scream burst from his throat, but

it was smothered before it was finished as the black shape of slime fastened upon him with irresistible force.

Giles Gowse—"Old Man" Gowse—got out of bed after eight hours of fitful tossing and intermittent nightmares and grouchily brewed coffee in the kitchen of his dilapidated farmhouse on the edge of Wharton's Swamp. Half the night, it seemed, the strench of stale sea water had permeated the house. His interrupted sleep had been full of foreboding, full of shadowy and evil portents.

Muttering to himself, he finished breakfast, took a milk pail from the pantry and started for the barn where he kept his single cow.

As he approached the barn, the strange offensive odor which had plagued him during the night assailed his nostrils anew.

"Wharton's Swamp! That's what it is!" he told himself. And he shook his fist at it.

When he entered the barn the stench was stronger than ever. Scowling, he strode toward the rickety stall where he kept the cow, Sarey.

Then he stood still and stared. Sarey was gone. The stall was empty.

He reentered the barnyard. "Sarey!" he called.

Rushing back into the barn, he inspected the stall. The rancid reek of the sea was strong here, and now he noticed a kind of shine on the floor. Bending closer, he saw that it was a slick coat of glistening slime as if some unspeakable creature covered with ooze had crept in and out of the stall.

This discovery, coupled with the weird disappearance of Sarey, was too much for his jangled nerves. With a wild yell he ran out of the barn and started for Clinton Center, two miles away.

His reception in the town enraged him. When he tried to tell people about the disappearance of his cow, Sarey, about the reek of sea and ooze in his barn the night before, they laughed at him. The more impolite ones, that is. Most of the others patiently heard him out—and then winked and touched their heads significantly when he was out of sight.

One man, the druggist, Jim Jelinson, seemed mildly interested. He said that as he was coming through his backyard from the garage late the previous evening, he had heard a fearful shriek somewhere in the distant darkness. It might, he averred, have come from the direction of Wharton's Swamp. But it had not been repeated, and eventually he had dismissed it from his mind.

When Old Man Gowse started for home late in the afternoon, he was filled with sullen, resentful bitterness. They thought he was crazy, eh? Well, Sarey *was* gone; they couldn't explain *that* away, could they? They explained the smell by saying it was dead fish cast up by the big wave which had washed into the swamp during the storm. Well—maybe. And the slime on his barn floor they said was snails. *Snails!* As if any snail he'd ever seen could cause that much slime.

As he was nearing home, he met Rupert Barnaby, his nearest neighbor. Rupert was carrying a rifle and he was accompanied by Jibbe, his hound.

Although there had been an element of bad blood between the two bachelor neighbors for some time, Old Man Gowse, much to Barnaby's surprise, nodded and stopped.

"Evenin' hunt, neighbor?"

Barnaby nodded. "Thought Jibbe might start up a coon. Moon later, likely."

"My cow's gone," Old Man Gowse said abruptly. "If you should see her—" He paused. "But I don't think you will. . . ."

Barnaby, bewildered, stared at him. "What you gettin' at?"

Old Man Gowse repeated what he had been telling all day in Clinton Center.

He shook his head when he finished, adding: "I wouldn't go huntin' in that swamp tonight fur—ten thousand dollars!"

Rupert Barnaby threw back his head and laughed. He was a big man, muscular, resourceful, and level-headed—little given to even mild flights of the imagination.

"Gowse," he laughed, "no use you given' me those spook stories! Your cow just got loose and wandered off. Why, I ain't even seen a bobcat in that swamp for over a year."

Old Man Gowse set his lips in a grim line. "Maybe," he said, as he turned away, "you'll see suthin' worse than a wildcat in that swamp tonight."

Shaking his head, Barnaby took off after his impatient hound. Old Man Gowse was getting queer all right. One of these days he'd probably go off altogether and have to be locked up.

Jibbe ran ahead, sniffing, darting from one ditch to another. As twilight closed in, Barnaby angled off the main road onto a twisting path which led directly into Wharton's Swamp.

He loved hunting. He would rather tramp through the brush than sit home in an easy chair. And even if an evening's foray turned up nothing, he didn't particularly mind. Actually he made out quite well; at least half his meat supply consisted of the rabbits, racoons, and occasional deer which he brought down in Wharton's Swamp.

When the moon rose, he was deep in the swamp. Twice Jibbe started off after rabbits, but both times he returned quickly, looking somewhat sheepish.

Something about his actions began to puzzle Barnaby. The dog seemed reluctant to move forward; he hung directly in front of the hunter. Once Barnaby tripped over him and nearly fell headlong.

The hunter paused finally, frowning, and looked ahead. The swamp appeared no different than usual. True, a rather offensive stench hung over it, but that was merely the result of the big waves which had splashed far inland during the recent storm. Probably an accumulation of seaweed and the decaying bodies of some dead fish lay rotting in the stagnant pools of the swamp.

Barnaby spoke sharply to the dog. "What ails you, boy? Git now! You trip me again, you'll get a boot."

The dog started ahead some distance, but with an air of reluctance. He sniffed the clumps of marsh grass in a perfunctory manner and seemed to have lost interest in the hunt.

Barnaby grew exasperated. Even when they discovered the fresh track of a racoon in the soft mud near a little pool, Jibbe manifested only slight interest.

He did run on a little further however, and Barnaby began to hope that, as they closed in, he would regain his customary enthusiasm.

In this he was mistaken. As they approached a thickly wooded area, latticed with tree thorns and covered with a heavy growth of cattails, the dog suddenly crouched in the shadows and refused to budge.

Barnaby was sure that the racoon had taken refuge in the nearby thickets. The dog's unprecedented conduct infuriated him.

After a number of sharp cuffs, Jibbe arose stiffly and moved ahead, the hair on his neck bristled up like a lion's mane.

Swearing to himself, Barnaby pushed into the darkened thickets after him.

It was quite black under the trees, in spite of the moonlight, and he moved cautiously in order to avoid stepping into a pool.

Suddenly, with a frantic yelp of terror, Jibbe liberally darted between his legs and shot out of the thickets. He ran on, howling weirdly as he went.

For the first time that evening Barnaby experienced a thrill of fear. In all his previous experience, Jibbe had never turned tail. On one occasion he had even plunged in after a good-sized bear.

Scowling into the deep darkness, Barnaby could see nothing. There were no baleful eyes glaring at him.

As his own eyes tried to penetrate the surrounding blackness, he recalled Old Man Gowse's warning with a bitter grimace. If the old fool happened to spot Jibbe streaking out of the swamp, Barnaby would never hear the end of it.

The thought of this angered him. He pushed on now with a feeling of sullen rage for whatever had terrified the dog. A good rifle shot would solve the mystery.

All at once he stopped and listened. From the darkness immediately ahead, he detected an odd sound, as if a large bulk were being dragged over the cattails.

He hesitated, unable to see anything, stoutly resisting an idiotic impulse to flee. The black darkness and the slimy stench of stagnant pools here in the thickets seemed to be suffocating him.

His heart began to pound as the slithering noise came closer. Every instinct told him to turn and run, but a kind of desperate stubbornness held him rooted to the spot.

The sound grew louder, and suddenly he was positive that something deadly and formidable was rushing toward him through the thickets with accelerated speed.

Throwing up his rifle, he pointed at the direction of the sound and fired.

In the brief flash of the rifle he saw something black and enormous and glistening, like a great flapping hood, break through the final thicket. It seemed to be *rolling* toward him, and it was moving with nightmare swiftness.

He wanted to scream and run, but even as the horror rushed forward, he understood that flight at this point would be futile. Even though the blood seemed to have congealed in his veins, he held the rifle pointed up and kept on firing.

The shots had no more visible effect than so many pebbles launched from a slingshot. At the last instant his nerve broke and he tried to escape, but the monstrous hood lunged upon him, flapped over him and squeezed, and his attempt at a scream turned into a tiny gurgle in his throat.

Old Man Gowse got up early after another uneasy night and walked out to inspect the barnyard area. Nothing further seemed amiss, but there was still no sign of Sarey. And that detestable odor arose from the direction of Wharton's Swamp when the wind was right.

After breakfast, Gowse set out for Rupert Barnaby's place, a mile or so distant along the road. He wasn't sure himself what he expected to find.

When he reached Barnaby's small but neat frame house, all was quiet. Too quiet. Usually Barnaby was up and about soon after sunrise.

On a sudden impulse, Gowse walked up the path and rapped on the front door. He waited and there was no reply. He knocked again and, after another pause, stepped off the porch.

Jibbe, Barnaby's hound, slunk around the side of the house. Ordinarily he would bound about and bark. But today he stood motionless—or nearly so—he was trembling—and stared at Gowse. The dog had a cowed, frightened, guilty air which was entirely alien to him.

"Where's Rup?" Gowse called to him. "Go get Rup!"

Instead of starting off, the dog threw back his head and emitted an eerie, long-drawn howl.

Gowse shivered. With a backward glance at the silent house, he started off down the road.

Now maybe they'd listen to him, he thought

grimly. They had laughed about the disappearance of Sarey; maybe they wouldn't laugh so easily when he told them that Rupert Barnaby had gone into Wharton's Swamp with his dog—and that the dog had come back alone.

When Police Chief Miles Underbeck saw Old Man Gowse come into headquarters in Clinton Center, he sat back and sighed heavily. He was busy this morning and undoubtedly Old Man Gowse was coming in to inquire about the infernal cow of his that had wandered off.

The old eccentric had a new and startling report, however. He claimed that Rupert Barnaby was missing. He'd gone into the swamp the night before, Gowse insisted, and had not returned.

When Chief Underbeck questioned him closely, Gowse admitted that he wasn't *positive* Barnaby hadn't returned. It was barely possible that he had returned home very early in the morning and then left again before Gowse arrived.

But Gowse fixed his flashing eyes on the Chief and shook his head. "He never came out, I tell ye! That dog of his knows. Howled, he did, like a dog howls for the dead. Whatever come and took Sarey—got Barnaby in the swamp last night!"

Chief Underbeck was not an excitable man. Gowse's outburst irritated him and left him unimpressed.

Somewhat gruffly he promised to look into the matter if Barnaby had not turned up by evening. Barnaby, he pointed out, knew the swamp better than anyone else in the county. And he was perfectly capable of taking care of himself. Probably, the Chief suggested, he had sent the dog home and gone elsewhere after finishing his hunt the evening before. The chances were he'd be back by suppertime.

Old Man Gowse shook his head with a kind of fatalistic skepticism. Vouching that events would soon prove his fears well founded, he shambled out of the station.

The day passed and there was no sign of Rupert Barnaby. At six o'clock, Old Man Gowse grimly marched into the Crown, Clinton Center's second-rate hotel, and registered for a room. At seven o'clock Chief Underbeck dispatched a prowl car to Barnaby's place. He waited impatiently for its return, drumming on the desk, disinterestedly shuffling through a sheaf of reports which had accumulated during the day.

The prowl car returned shortly before eight. Sergeant Grimes made his report. "Nobody there, sir. Place locked up tight. Searched the grounds. All we saw was Barnaby's dog. Howled and ran off as if the devil were on his tail!"

Chief Underbeck was troubled. If Barnaby *was* missing, a search should be started at once. But it was already getting dark, and portions of Wharton's Swamp were very nearly impassible even during the day. Besides, there was no proof that Barnaby had not gone off for a visit, perhaps to nearby Stantonville, for instance, to call on a crony and stay overnight.

By nine o'clock he had decided to postpone any action till morning. A search now would probably be futile in any case. The swamp offered too many obstacles. If Barnaby had not turned up by morning, and there was no report that he had been seen elsewhere, a systematic search of the marsh could begin.

Not long after he had arrived at his decision, and as he was somewhat wearily preparing to leave headquarters and go home, a new and genuinely alarming interruption took place.

Shortly before nine-thirty, a car braked to a sudden stop outside headquarters. An elderly man hurried in, supporting by the arm a sobbing, hysterical young girl. Her skirt and stockings were torn and there were a number of scratches on her face.

After assisting her to a chair, the man turned to Chief Underbeck and the other officers who gathered around.

"Picked her up on the highway out near Wharton's Swamp. Screaming at the top of her lungs!" He wiped his forehead. "She ran right in front of my car. Missed her by a miracle. She was so crazy with fear I couldn't make sense out of what she said. Seems like something grabbed her boy friend in the bushes out there. Anyway, I got her in the car without much trouble and I guess I broke a speed law getting here."

Chief Underbeck surveyed the man keenly. He was obviously shaken himself, and since he did not appear to be concealing anything, the Chief turned to the girl.

He spoke soothingly, doing his best to reassure her, and at length she composed herself sufficiently to tell her story.

Her name was Dolores Rell and she lived in nearby Stantonville. Earlier in the evening she had gone riding with her fiance, Jason Bukmeist of Clinton Center. As Jason was driving along the highway adjacent to Wharton's Swamp, she had remarked that the early evening moonlight looked very romantic over the marsh. Jason had stopped the car, and after they had surveyed the scene for some minutes, he suggested that since the evening was warm, a brief "stroll in the moonlight" might be fun.

Dolores had been reluctant to leave the car, but at length had been persuaded to take a short walk along the edge of the marsh where the terrain was relatively firm.

As the couple were walking along under the trees, perhaps twenty yards or so from the car, Dolores became aware of an unpleasant odor and wanted to turn back. Jason, however, told her she only imagined it and insisted on going further. As the trees grew closer together, they walked Indian file, Jason taking the lead.

Suddenly, she said, they both heard something swishing through the brush toward them. Jason told her not to be frightened, that it was probably someone's cow. As it came closer, however, it seemed to be moving with incredible speed. And it didn't seem to be making the kind of noise a cow would make.

At the last second Jason whirled with a cry of fear and told her to run. Before she could move, she saw a monstrous something rushing under the trees in the dim moonlight. For an instant she stood rooted with horror; then she turned and ran. She thought she heard Jason running behind her. She couldn't be sure. But immediately after, she heard him scream.

In spite of her terror, she turned and looked behind her.

At this point in her story she became hysterical again and several minutes passed before she could go on.

She could not describe exactly what she had seen as she looked over her shoulder. The thing which she had glimpsed rushing under the trees had caught up with Jason. It almost completely covered him. All she could see of him was his agonized face and part of one arm, low near the ground, as if the thing were squatting astride him. She could not say what it was. It was black, formless, bestial, and yet not bestial. It was the dark gliding indescribable kind of horror which she had shuddered at when she was a little girl alone in the nursery at night.

She shuddered now and covered her eyes as she tried to picture what she had seen. "O God—*the darkness came alive! The darkness came alive!*"

Somehow, she went on when calmer, she had stumbled through the trees into the road. She was so terrified she hardly noticed the approaching car.

There could be no doubt that Dolores Rell was in the grip of genuine terror. Chief Underbeck acted with alacrity. After the ashen-faced girl had been driven to a nearby hospital for treatment of her scratches and the administration of a sedative, Underbeck rounded up all available men on the force, equipped them with shot guns, rifles and flashlights, hurried them into four prowl cars, and started off for Wharton's Swamp.

Jason Bukmeist's car was found where he had parked it. It had not been disturbed. A search of the nearby swamp area, conducted in the glare of flashlights, proved fruitless. Whatever had attacked Bukmeist had apparently carried him off into the farthest recesses of the sprawling swamp.

After two futile hours of brush breaking and marsh sloshing, Chief Underbeck wearily rounded up his men and called off the hunt until morning.

As the first faint streaks of dawn appeared in the sky over Wharton's Swamp, the search began again. Reinforcements, including civilian volunteers from Clinton Center, had arrived, and a systematic combing of the entire swamp commenced.

By noon, the search had proved fruitless—or nearly so. One of the searchers brought in a battered hat and a rye whisky bottle which he had discovered on the edge of the marsh under a sweet-gum tree. The shapeless felt hat was old and worn, but it was dry. It had, therefore, apparently been discarded in the swamp since the storm of a few days ago. The whisky bottle looked new; in fact, a few drops of rye remained in it. The searcher reported that the remains of a small campfire were also found under the sweet gum.

In the hope that this evidence might have some bearing on the disappearance of Jason Bukmeist, Chief Underbeck ordered a canvass of every liquor store in Clinton Center in an attempt to learn the names of everyone who had recently purchased a bottle of the particular brand of rye found under the tree.

The search went on, and mid-afternoon brought another, more ominous discovery. A diligent searcher, investigating a trampled area in a large growth of cattails, picked a rifle out of the mud.

After the slime and dirt had been wiped away, two of the searchers vouched that it belonged to Rupert Barnaby. One of them had hunted with him and remembered a bit of scrollwork on the rifle stock.

While Chief Underbeck was uneasily weighing this bit of evidence, a report of the liquor store canvass in Clinton Center arrived. Every recent purchaser of a quart bottle of the particular brand in question had been investigated. Only one could not be located—a tramp who had hung around the town for several days and had been ordered out.

By evening most of the exhausted searching party were convinced that the tramp, probably in a state of homicidal viciousness brought on by drink, had murdered both Rupert Barnaby and Jason and secreted their bodies in one of the deep pools of the swamp. The chances were the murderer was still sleeping off the effects of drink somewhere in the tangled thickets of the marsh.

Most of the searchers regarded Dolores Rell's melodramatic story with a great deal of skepticism. In the dim moonlight, they pointed out, a frenzied, wild-eyed tramp bent on imminent murder might very well have resembled some kind of monster. And the girl's hysteria had probably magnified what she had seen.

As night closed over the dismal morass, Chief Underbeck reluctantly suspended the hunt. In view of the fact that the murderer probably still lurked in the woods, however, he decided to establish a system of all-night patrols along the highway which paralleled the swamp. If the quarry lay hidden in the treacherous tangle of trees and brush, he would not be able to escape onto the highway without running into one of the patrols. The only other means of egress from the swamp lay miles across the mire where the open sea washed against a reedy beach. And it was quite unlikely that the fugitive would even attempt escape in that direction.

The patrols were established in three hour shifts, two men to a patrol, both heavily armed and both equipped with powerful searchlights. They were ordered to investigate every sound or movement which they detected in the brush bordering the highway. After a single command to halt, they were to shoot to kill. Any curious motorists who stopped to inquire about the hunt were to be swiftly waved on their way after being warned not to give rides to anyone and to report all hitchhikers.

Fred Storr and Luke Matson, on the midnight to three o'clock patrol, passed an uneventful two hours on their particular stretch of the highway. Matson finally sat down on a fallen tree stump a few yards from the edge of the road.

"Legs givin' out," he commented wryly, resting his rifle on the stump. "Might as well sit a few minutes."

Fred Storr lingered nearby. "Guess so, Luke. Don't look like—" Suddenly he scowled into the black fringes of the swamp. "You hear something, Luke?"

Luke listened, twisting around on the stump. "Well, maybe," he said finally, "kind of a little scratchy sound like."

He got up, retrieving his rifle.

"Let's take a look," Fred suggested in a low voice. He stepped over the stump and Luke followed him toward the tangle of brush which marked the border of the swamp jungle.

Several yards further along they stopped again. The sound became more audible. It was a kind of slithering, scraping sound, such as might be produced by a heavy body dragging itself over uneven ground.

"Sounds like—a snake," Luke ventured. "A damn big snake!"

"We'll get a little closer," Fred whispered. "You be ready with that gun when I switch on my light!"

They moved ahead a few more yards. Then a powerful yellow ray stabbed into the thickets ahead as Fred switched on his flashlight. The ray searched the darkness, probing in one direction and then another.

Luke lowered his rifle a little, frowning. "Don't see a thing," he said. "Nothing but a big pool of black scum up ahead there."

Before Fred had time to reply, the pool of black scum reared up into horrible life. In one hideous second it hunched itself into a glistening hood and rolled forward with fearful speed.

Luke Matson screamed and fired simultaneously as the monstrous scarf of slime shot forward. A moment later it swayed above him. He fired again and the thing fell upon him.

In avoiding the initial rush of the horror, Fred Storr lost his footing. He fell headlong—and turned just in time to witness a sight which slowed the blood in his veins.

The monster had pounced upon Luke Matson. Now, as Fred watched, paralyzed with horror, it spread itself over and around the form of Luke until he was completely enveloped. The faint writhing of his limbs could still be seen. Then the thing squeezed, swelling into a hood and flattening itself again, and the writhing ceased.

As soon as the thing lifted and swung forward in his direction, Fred Storr, goaded by frantic fear, overcame the paralysis which had frozen him.

Grabbing the rifle which had fallen beside him, he aimed it at the shape of living slime and started firing. Pure terror possessed him as he saw that the shots were having no effect. The thing lunged toward him, to all visible appearances entirely oblivious to the rifle slugs tearing into its loathsome viscid mass.

Acting out of some instinct which he himself could not have named, Fred Storr dropped the rifle and seized his flashlight, playing its powerful beam directly upon the onrushing horror.

The thing stopped, scant feet away, and appeared to hesitate. It slid quickly aside at an angle, but Storr followed it immediately with the cone of light. It backed up finally and flattened out, as if trying by that means to avoid the light, but he trained the beam on it steadily, sensing with every primitive fiber which he possessed that the yellow shaft of light was the one thing which held off hideous death.

Now there were shouts in the nearby darkness and other lights began stabbing the shadows. Members of the adjacent patrols, alarmed by the sound of rifle fire, had come running to investigate.

Suddenly the nameless horror squirmed quickly out of the flashlight's beam and rushed away in the darkness.

In the leaden light of early dawn Chief Underbeck climbed into a police car waiting on the highway near Wharton's Swamp and headed back for Clinton Center. He had made a decision and he was grimly determined to act on it at once.

When he reached headquarters, he made two telephone calls in quick succession, one to the governor of the state and the other to the commander of the nearby Camp Evans Military Reservation.

The horror in Wharton's Swamp—he had decided—could not be handled by the limited men and resources at his command.

Rupert Barnaby, Jason Bukmeist and Luke Matson had without any doubt perished in the swamp. The anonymous tramp, it now began to appear, far from being the murderer, had been only one more victim. And Fred Storr—well, he hadn't disappeared. But the other patrol members had found him sitting on the ground near the edge of the swamp in the clutches of a mind-warping fear which had, temporarily at least, reduced him to near idiocy. Hours after he had been taken home and put to bed, he had refused to loosen his grip on a flashlight which he squeezed in one hand. When they switched the flashlight off, he screamed, and they had to switch it on again. His story was so wildly melodramatic it could scarcely be accepted by rational minds. And yet—they had said as much about Dolores Rell's hysterical account. And Fred Storr was no excitable young girl; he had a reputation for level-headedness, stolidity, and verbal honesty which was touched with understatement rather than exaggeration. As Chief Underbeck arose and walked out to his car in order to start back to Wharton's Swamp, he noticed Old man Gowse coming down the block.

With a sudden thrill of horror he remembered the eccentric's missing cow. Before the old man came abreast, he had slammed the car door and issued crisp directions to the waiting driver. As the car sped away, he glanced in the rear-view mirror.

Old Man Gowse stood grimly motionless on the walk in front of police headquarters.

"Old Man Cassandra," Chief Underbeck muttered. The driver shot a swift glance at him and stepped on the gas.

Less than two hours after Chief Underbeck arrived at Wharton's Swamp, the adjacent highway was crowded with cars—state police cars, cars of the local curious, and Army trucks from Camp Evans.

Promptly at nine o'clock over three hundred soldiers, police and citizen volunteers, all armed, swung into the swamp to begin a careful search.

Shortly before dusk most of them had arrived at the sea on the far side of the swamp. Their exhaustive efforts had netted nothing. One soldier, noticing fierce eyes glaring out of a tree, had bagged an owl, and one of the state policemen had flushed a young bobcat. Someone else had stepped on a copperhead and been treated for snakebite. But there was no sign of a monster, a murderous tramp, nor any of the missing men.

In the face of mounting skepticism, Chief Underbeck stood firm. Pointing out that so far as they knew to date the murderer prowled only at night, he ordered that after a four-hour rest and meal period the search should continue.

A number of helicopters which had hovered over the area during the afternoon landed on the strip of shore, bringing food and supplies. At Chief Underbeck's insistence, barriers were set up on the beach. Guards were stationed along the entire length of the highway; powerful searchlights were brought up. Another truck from Camp Evans arrived with a portable machine gun and several flame throwers.

By eleven o'clock that night the stage was set. The beach barriers were in place, guards were at station, and huge searchlights, erected near the highway, swept the dismal marsh with probing cones of light.

At eleven-fifteen the night patrols, each consisting of ten strongly armed men, struck into the swamp again.

Ravenous with hunger, the hood of horror reared out of the mud at the bottom of a rancid pool and rose toward the surface. Flopping ashore in the darkness, it slid quickly away over the clumps of scattered swamp grass. It was impelled, as always, by a savage and enormous hunger.

Although hunting in its new environment had been good, its immense appetite knew no appeasement. The more food it consumed, the more it seemed to require.

As it rushed off, alert to the minute vibrations which indicated food, it became aware of various disturbing emanations. Although it was the time of darkness in this strange world, the darkness at this usual hunting period was oddly pierced by the monster's hated enemy—light. The food vibrations were stronger than the shape of slime had ever experienced. They were on all sides, powerful, purposeful, moving in many directions all through the lower layers of puzzling, light-riven darkness.

Lifting out of the ooze, the hood of horror flowed up a latticework of gnarled swamp snags and hung motionless, while drops of muddy water rolled off its glistening surface and dripped below. The thing's sensory apparatus told it that the maddening streaks of lack-of-darkness were everywhere.

Even as it hung suspended on the snags like a great filthy carpet coated with slime, a terrible touch of light slashed through the surrounding darkness and burned against it.

It immediately loosened its hold on the snags and fell back into the ooze with a mighty *plop*. Nearby, the vibrations suddenly increased in intensity. The maddening streamers of light shot through the darkness on all sides.

Baffled and savage, the thing plunged into the ooze and propelled itself in the opposite direction.

But this proved to be only a temporary respite. The vibrations redoubled in intensity. The darkness almost disappeared, replaced by bolts and rivers of light.

For the first time in its incalculable existence, the thing experienced something vaguely akin to fear. The light could not be snatched up and squeezed and smothered to death. It was an alien enemy against which the hood of horror had learned only one defense—flight, hiding.

And now as its world of darkness was torn apart by sudden floods and streamers of light, the monster instinctively sought the refuge afforded by that vast black cradle from which it had climbed.

Flinging itself through the swamp, it headed back for sea.

The guard patrols stationed along the beach, roused by the sound of gunfire and urgent shouts of warning from the interior of the swamp, stood or knelt with ready weapons as the clamor swiftly approached the sea.

The dismal reedy beach lay fully exposed in the harsh glare of searchlights. Waves rolled in toward shore, splashing white crests of foam far up on the sands. In the searchlight's illumination the dark waters glistened with an oily iridescence.

The shrill cries increased. The watchers tensed, waiting. And suddenly across the long dreary flats clotted with weed stalks and sunken drifts there burst into view a nightmare shape which froze the shore patrols in their tracks.

A thing of slimy blackness, a thing which had no essential shape, no discernible earthly features, rushed through the thorn thickets and onto the flats. It was a shape of utter darkness, one second a great flapping hood, the next a black viscid pool of living ooze which flowed upon itself, sliding forward with incredible speed.

Some of the guards remained rooted where they stood, too overcome with horror to pull the triggers of their weapons. Others broke the spell of terror and began firing. Bullets from half a dozen rifles tore into the black monster speeding across the mud flats.

As the thing neared the end of the flats and approached the first sand dunes of the open beach, the patrol guards who had flushed it from the swamp broke into the open.

One of them paused, bellowing at the beach guards. "It's heading for sea! For God's sake don't let it escape!"

The beach guards redoubled their firing, suddenly realizing with a kind of sick horror that the monster was apparently unaffected by the rifle slugs. Without

a single pause, it rolled through the last fringe of cattails and flopped onto the sands.

As in a hideous nightmare, the guards saw it flap
over the nearest sand dune and slide toward the sea.
A moment later however, they remembered the
barbed wire beach barrier which Chief Underbeck
had stubbornly insisted on their erecting.

Gaining heart, they closed in, running over the
dunes toward the spot where the black horror would
strike the wire.

Someone in the lead yelled in sudden triumph.
"It's caught! It's stuck on the wire!"

The searchlights concentrated swaths of light on
the barrier.

The thing had reached the barbed wire fence and
apparently flung itself against the twisted strands.
Now it appeared to be hopelessly caught; it twisted
and flopped and squirmed like some unspeakable
giant jellyfish snared in a fisherman's net.

The guards ran forward, sure of their victory. All
at once, however, the guard in the lead screamed a
wild warning. "It's squeezing through! It's getting
away!"

In the glare of light they saw with consternation
that the monster appeared to be *flowing* through the
wire like a blob of liquescent ooze.

Ahead lay a few yards of downward slanting
beach and, beyond that, rolling breakers of the open
sea.

There was a collective gasp of horrified dismay as
the monster, with a quick forward lurch, squeezed
through the barrier. It tilted there briefly, twisting, as
if a few last threads of itself might still be entangled
in the wire.

As it moved to disengage itself and rush down the
wet sands into the black sea, one of the guards hurled
himself forward until he was almost abreast of the
barrier. Sliding to his knees, he aimed at the escaping
hood of horror.

A second later a great searing spout of flame shot from his weapon and burst in a smoky red blossom against the thing on the opposite side of the wire.

Black oily smoke billowed into the night. A ghastly stench flowed over the beach. The guards saw a flaming mass of horror grope away from the barrier. The soldier who aimed the flame thrower held it remorselessly steady.

There was a hideous bubbling, hissing sound. Vast gouts of thick, greasy smoke swirled into the night air. The indescribable stench became almost unbearable.

When the soldier finally shut off the flame thrower, there was nothing in sight except the white-hot glowing wires of the barrier and a big patch of blackened sand.

With good reason the mantle of slime had hated light, for the source of light is fire—the final unknown enemy which even the black hood could not drag down and devour.

Joseph Payne Brennan was born in Bridgeport Conn. on December 20, 1918. A few weeks later his family moved back to New Haven where he has lived ever since. Brennan was forced to leave college in his sophomore year because of an illness in the family. He worked on a local newspaper for three years and spent another year writing movie reviews for *Theatre News*. He began working at the Yale University Library in 1941. Two years later he was posted to active duty in Patton's Third Army, 26th ("Yankee") Division. Before he resumed his career as Acquisitions Assistant at Yale in 1946, Brennan had earned five army battle stars. His first book, a collection of poems entitled *Heart of Earth*, was published by Decker Press in 1950. He has subsequently published twelve more books, either short-story or poetry collections. His most recent work, ACT OF PROVIDENCE, written in collaboration with Donald M. Grant, was published in 1979.

Short stories and/or poems have been reprinted in well over a hundred anthologies and translated into French, German, Dutch, Spanish and many other languages. Two stories, *The Pool* and *Goodbye, Mr. Bliss*, were filmed for the old TV "Thriller" show; others have been adapted for radio. *The Calamander Chest*, originally published in *Weird Tales*, was recorded by Vincent Price for Caedmon.

Books by Joseph Payne Brennan

SHORT STORY COLLECTIONS

Nine Horrors and a Dream	(Arkham House 1958)
The Dark Returners	(Macabre House 1959)
Scream at Midnight	(Macabre House 1963)
Stories of Darkness and Dread	(Arkham House 1973)
The Casebook of Lucius Leffing	(Macabre House 1973)
The Chronicles of Lucius Leffing	(Donald M. Grant 1977)

NOVELETTE

Act of Providence (in collaboration with Donald M. Grant)
    (Donald M. Grant 1979)

POETRY COLLECTIONS

Heart of Earth	(Decker Press 1950)
The Humming Stair	(Big Mountain Press 1953)
The Wind of Time	(Hawk & Whipporwill Press 1961)
Nightmare Need	(Arkham House 1964)
Edges of Night	(Pilot Press 1974)
Webs of Time	(Macabre House 1979)